MARRY M

Sister Laura Bradfield has a very hard time when
she agrees to work with handsome but unpopular
Doctor Warwick. Things go from bad to worse,
but not before she discovers she is falling in love
. . .

MARRY ME, STRANGER

BY

ANNE VINTON

MILLS & BOON LIMITED
London . Sydney . Toronto

First published in Great Britain 1971
by Mills & Boon Limited, 15–16 Brook's Mews,
London W1A 1DR

This edition 1981
Australian copyright 1981
Philippine copyright 1981

ISBN 0 263 73463 3

Set in 10 on 10½ pt. Monophoto Baskerville

Made and printed in Great Britain by
Richard Clay (The Chaucer Press) Ltd.,
Bungay, Suffolk

CHAPTER ONE

LAURA BRADFIELD often wondered why she was tempted to take walks in weather that made other people curl up by warm fires and toast their toes, or slip into cafés and imbibe hot, refreshing drinks. Whenever it thundered, or blew a gale, or rained cats and dogs—providing she was free—Laura donned mac and scarf and mittens and marched off, turning her face in a kind of glory towards the elements. She enjoyed being buffeted and lightning made such pretty patterns in a dark sky that she forgot to be afraid, and rain was really so clean and refreshing. If it was good for grass and flowers, then why not people?

She had arrived in Thornsea only that afternoon; had desultorily explored her antiseptic but dull room in the Nurses' Home of the local cottage hospital, and feeling her feet tingling, as soon as the late September equinoctial gale struck the town, she had decided on an evening walk along the cliffs.

It was really wild and she had tied a blue headscarf over her fair hair, which looked so unusual with her large, luminous brown eyes. She had recently been working far inland, a day's journey from any coast, and found her present surroundings picturesque.

Thornsea wasn't exactly a seaside resort; it had no beach, for one thing, only boulders and sharp-toothed rocks which had been gouged in pre-history out of the sharp cliffs. There was a harbour at the far end of the town and a fishing fleet which supplied a frozen-food firm. The air was cold and clean and invigorating.

Laura loved walking and often walked alone. Not many nurses, she quite understood, felt like walks after their long hours on duty. Her friends used to protest, 'Good lord, Laura, haven't you had enough? Anyway, it's raining.'

But walking in the rain was conducive to thinking and she always felt refreshed by her excursions. Sitting in stuffy common-rooms where half the inmates smoked made one feel as dull and heavy as lead.

So noisy was the wind that she thought she must be mistaken in thinking she had heard a human voice crying out. Why, there were demons in that wind, shrieking and trying to tear the scarf from her head. She laughed in their teeth and then she heard one of the demons speak.

'Is anybody there? Help!'

There was no demon, but a human being in trouble. She couldn't see anyone but called 'coo-ee!' as loudly as she could.

'Here! Here!'

She leaned into the wind over the cliff edge and saw a man lying on a ledge further down.

'Hello!' she called. 'In trouble?'

'Get down,' he said curtly, 'or you'll be blown over. Are you capable of taking simple instructions? If not I would be obliged if you could just go and get help.'

She felt stung and replied, as she flattened herself out on the edge of the cliff, 'I may be mistaken, of course, but I think I'm quite capable. Are you hurt?'

'No, I am not hurt. It may not be obvious to you from up there, but I'm hanging on to a boy with a broken leg. He's unconscious, I think. He was swinging on a rope, after sea-gull nests, and was dashed against the cliff. I have the rope round my wrist and its damned near broken. My wrist, I mean. Can you drive a car?'

'Yes, but——'

'Well, my car's about a hundred yards along the cliff. Bring it broadside behind that boulder up there, then get the tow rope out of the boot, secure it well to the towing bar and drop it over here.'

'Oh, dear! Oh, dear!——' Laura almost wailed.

'This is no time for asking what can the matter be,' the man said testily. 'Please do something or get someone else quickly.'

Laura had no time to think she didn't like the creature very much, but ran along the cliff-top to where an old Jaguar Mark Ten was parked. She had never driven a big car, only a Volkswagen and a Mini, but seeing the keys were in the ignition she decided she had better have a go. As she put her foot on the accelerator the powerful car lurched forward, almost carrying her, too, to disaster, but she slammed on the brakes, hard, and then got the feel of the great monster and crept along the cliff sward until she was behind a very solid-looking boulder. She needed the keys for the boot, and now her wrist was beginning to ache in sympathy with the man's over the cliff. She often suffered her patient's pains, too. It was something to do with a powerful imagination which was not exactly an asset in a good nurse, as many of her superiors had told her. Facts were all that were important in dealing with sick and broken human bodies.

She could scarcely handle the thick towing rope, it was so heavy, but she saw that there was a hook on the towing bar and a loop on the rope and somehow she connected the two and wrapped the rope round once more for safety. Then, with a struggle in the teeth of the gale, she dropped the rope over the edge and scrambled down to the shelf herself, sinking to her knees.

'I—thought you'd gone for a cup of tea or something,' the man said ungratefully.

'Don't be rude!' she flared back. 'I'm here and I've done as you asked, so let's get on with it.'

She was sorry she had snapped at him when she saw his teeth clenched in pain. They must have seemed very long moments to him.

'The rope's very firm, I assure you,' she told him. 'Please tell me what else to do.'

Obeying his instructions, she tied a slip-knot in the rope and left a wide loop. She then had to manoeuvre this under the dangling boy's feet until it could be drawn up under his arms and tightened. She drew the loop taut,

7

hoping her knot would stand the test, and at last her companion was able to release his hold and relax his strained, bloodless hand and wrist. She then had to scramble back to the cliff-top again and drive the car slowly, using the boulder as a belaying pin, until the boy was safely beside her. Looking over the cliff again, she asked, 'Are *you* all right?'

'Unfortunately not,' he said tersely. 'I'm sorry to say I shall need your help to get up there.'

'Don't be sorry,' she told him. 'I may not be very big, but I'm tough.'

'Most women are, I find,' he actually smiled as she lent him her shoulder and put her strong young arm round his waist, 'as old leather.'

'That may not be so bad,' she retorted, 'so long as we don't look like old leather.'

'Well, we made it,' he said grudgingly, as they reached the top of the scramble path, and then some reaction made him stagger so that she grabbed at him afresh. 'You must think I'm providing the infirmity for the sake of the remedy,' he joked, 'but you couldn't be more wrong.'

'I gathered that,' she told him, really noting for the first time that he was younger than she had imagined—probably a little over thirty—and that his hair was black, his eyes piercingly blue. 'I think we can conclude from your remarks in general that I was the very last person you would have preferred to come to your aid. I only hope I have acquitted myself adequately, even in your sight.'

'Ahem!' he replied to this, tongue in cheek. 'Even after that I still have to admit I need you. We—or rather you—have to get a splint on that leg, drive us to the nearest phone, get the ambulance and drive me home.' He held up his wrist which was now swollen, black with bruising. 'I'd be a risk on my own.'

He told her there was a doctor's bag in the car and there were bandages in it.

'So he's a doctor, is he?' she asked herself. 'I must

8

watch I never meet him socially.—Not that he seems like a social type, just a good-looking sourpuss.'

They used golf-clubs for splints and the man remarked that the boy's pulse was fine.

'He's put himself into the land of Erewhon, which was a good thing for us. If he'd been yelling and struggling we'd both have probably been dead on those rocks by now.'

'Obviously the gods don't love you,' Laura remarked innocently.

'*You* needn't tell me that, miss, madam, whatever you are,' he said bitterly. 'I don't expect to impress in heaven where I've failed on earth. Now can we get the poor kid in the back seat and move on, do you think? I don't think I ever saw so many thumbs on one pair of small hands.'

Laura looked up angrily but didn't retort. She felt she would go up like a bomb if she once did really let go. Even when she was driving the car he was sighing and humming and ha-ing beside her as though she should automatically drive an unfamiliar vehicle with excellence. She stopped at a phone box at the edge of the town, asked for an ambulance and then had to call her companion to verify the emergency.

'Can't you even *do* that?' he asked her. 'What would happen if your house was on fire, I wonder!'

She waited to see the boy taken aboard the ambulance; the golf-clubs were so well fixed that the attendants left them on until they transferred him to the hospital Casualty Department. Laura then asked for directions to drive her companion home.

'You think you can make Easthope Terrace?' he asked. 'It means going through traffic.'

She said, 'If you confine your remarks to simple directions. I'll make it. I happen to be a stranger in these parts, believe it or not.'

They arrived at Easthope Terrace without further incident. The houses looked superior, though some had been converted into flats.

'Well, we made it,' the man said with an outsize sigh of what she took to be relief. 'Thank you, in case I omitted to say so earlier.'

'You've mentioned everything but that,' she accused him, standing on the pavement and smoothing herself down.

'Will you,' he asked more reasonably, 'come in for a cup of tea or something?'

She felt she had been waiting for such an opening and she couldn't resist taking her cue. Her chestnut eyes flashing, she said, 'No, thank you. So far as I'm concerned you can *get lost!*' and she stalked away into the gathering gloom of evening.

He stood for a moment watching the neatness of her ankles and smiled wryly. 'You do ask for it, boy,' he told himself, conscious of his wrist banging and burning quite unbearably, 'and by jiminy, do you get it!'

Laura donned her neat staff nurse's uniform, wondering if it would be considered suitable for Thornsea Cottage Hospital, and pinned a starched cap expertly on her plentiful fair hair, which she dressed up in a French roll for duty. She regarded herself in the spotted mirror, which she had wedged into place with an envelope. All the mirrors of her nursing career tilted either forward or backward of their own accord and they never seemed to register correctly. This one made her appear to have a swollen right cheek, but when she peeped in her hand-bag mirror she could confirm that it lied.

It was the first time she had had a room to herself, and though she had been glad of this on arrival, she now almost regretted it. Back at St Christopher's, her old hospital, at this time there would have been a merry gossip going on with her two room-mates telling of their previous evening's escapades, mostly of an amorous nature and not always strictly true. Laura had been the one who listened and exclaimed 'Really?' or 'I don't believe you, Trudy. Dr Richmond was on duty last night, because I saw him.'

She missed the gossiping but ambivalently enjoyed the privacy.

Just then someone tapped on her room door and as she called out two girls entered. One was palely pretty, with light-coloured brows and lashes, which usually denote poor sight; the other was dark as ebony with stubble hair and a wide, toothy grin.

'Good morning!' Laura greeted, tentatively holding out her hand.

'Hello!' greeted the fair girl, wringing her hand. 'You don't mind us dropping in? We heard you were new here. I'm Fay Barnes. This is Tundi Oluri, from Nigeria, but she answers to Bournville.'

'And you don't get three guesses why!' laughed the dusky girl. 'We thought maybe you were feeling lonely?'

'I was a bit,' Laura admitted, to be friendly rather than because it was true.

They asked where she was from and exchanged news of their training hospitals.

'Why did you come to a crummy place like Thornsea?' asked Fay. 'I live here, so that's my reason, and Bournville doesn't know any better. But a full staff nurse——?'

It was time to draw away from further intimacy, Laura decided with regret, so she said quietly, 'I have been acting-Sister for six months. That's what I've been offered here, and *I* think it's a nice little place.'

'Oh, I say, Sister, eh? Oh, well, no wonder you have a royal suite. We wondered, you see, because *we* all share.'

'So we better be goin',' said Bournville, looking suddenly watchful.

Laura kept the fixed smile on her face until they had left and closed her door and then she slumped suddenly on the bed. Strange how an innocent observation could bring everything back again and make her feel such an—outsider.

She wondered if she could afford to have close friends ever again; if it might not be better to be a lone she-wolf and keep her affairs to herself as much as was possible.

Friends expected to give, and receive, confidences, and Laura didn't want to talk about the past with anyone. She knew the exception must be Miss Trueblood, the Principal Nursing Officer of this little hospital—who was still, in spite of the authorities, addressed as Matron. But Matron had been told the bald facts already, and had still accepted her without loss of status. She might want to ask her own questions about that awful affair, but then—please God—it could be put away and forgotten, if one could ever forget one had been responsible for a patient's death.

Laura hadn't mentioned the previous evening's adventure to anyone. In fact she wasn't yet on speaking terms with anybody in the hospital, as they were all too busy flitting here and there and she was not the type to deliberately force herself on other people. She was to see Matron at a quarter to nine and be allotted her duties.

She still felt angry when she remembered that awful doctor person hustling and insulting her. What else could she have done in an emergency like that? She also felt rather hot-cheeked when she remembered her own rudeness on departing. Two wrongs would never make a right, but it was as though something had to pop or she would have burst. Maybe it was a legacy of hospital discipline, where the hierarchy could say what they liked to the lowly but must never be answered back. Many was the time Laura had stood looking meek, her hands clasped apparently demurely behind her, while some Sister or other questioned her intelligence and capabilities in the most sarcastic terms imaginable, and always one waited to be dismissed and responded quietly with 'Yes, Sister,' or 'Sorry, Sister,' when one would have loved to have joined battle and asked Sister if she had three 'A' levels, or did the work of three with only one pair of hands.

Though there had been some satisfaction in telling a strange doctor to 'Get lost', Laura naturally hoped she never saw the creature again. Whatever one never said to hospital Sisters applied doubly to medical staff; it was,

'Yes, sir; no, sir; three bags full, sir,' in a very big way, no matter what clots they might be.

The breakfast bell rang and Laura emerged from her room to find herself eyed, yet avoided, by a horde of blue-clad nurses. Obviously Nurse Barnes and Bournville had been busy. There were a few desultory 'Good mornings' and then a navy-blue-clad figure appeared, who said, 'I heard you were at the other end of my corridor, Sister. I was asked to watch out for you. You'll come to our table, of course. My name's Martyn, spelt with a y.'

'And mine's Bradfield.'

The two shook hands and walked along together down a long, connecting corridor to the hospital proper and the staff dining-room.

'You haven't brought your dark uniform?' asked Sister Martyn, who was plain, thin, sallow and about thirty.

'I was only acting-Sister at my last hospital. My ward Sister was ill for a long time, you see, so I had to carry on. Naturally I would like it to be made official before I dress the part.'

'Yes, indeed. Anyhow, I don't know whether it's significant, but I was asked to watch out for the new Sister,' and the older woman smiled. 'This is our table.'

Laura was introduced to an incredibly beautiful Pakistani Sister called Mahmoud, and an older woman, who looked due for retirement, whose name was Saunders.

'And we're the only residents,' Martyn proceeded, 'apart from Jenkins, who's on nights. She usually joins us for breakfast, so you'll be meeting her. There are two married Sisters, who live at home, naturally. Trevor is just a bit older than you and Jepson is a West Indian. Her husband's a lab assistant, though it's a shame, because he practised as a doctor back in Jamaica. It seems his qualifications just aren't good enough for our Health Service.'

Breakfast consisted of the usual hospital fare of thick, grey-looking porridge, hard streaky bacon and tomatoes and toast on the Sisters' table only; the nurses had to be content with doorsteps of bread with their marmalade. A shrill whistle blasted and the nurses rose as one, some of the hungrier ones grabbing unfinished bread and marmalade to take with them.

'We have a quarter of an hour's grace,' said Martyn. 'Time for a smoke, if you do, and a natter.'

The night Sister, as pale and austere as a nun, arrived just then and was introduced to Laura.

'I wonder where you'll go?' she pondered. 'There's Outpatients' and your ward, Saunders, and the orthopaedic wing——'

Martyn gave a little cough which sounded purely affected.

'I want her on my ward,' said Sister Saunders hastily, and Laura noticed how she had a peculiar nervous twitch, which made her appear to be shaking her head. 'I really am overworked. I'm Children,' she told Laura.

'Oh, how lovely! Actually I was on the orthopaedic ward as Staff, at my last hospital,' Laura told them. 'When I finished I was on a cardiac ward, but orthopaedics is my favourite.'

'Don't say that!' Martyn pleaded. 'Trevor will have a fit.'

'Why?' asked Laura.

'Because we're sort of boycotting the orthopaedic ward. We're having a feud with the senior orthopaedic surgeon.'

'Oh? Isn't that rather hard on the patients?'

'No. They're all right. Matron has to employ outside help from the agency. We simply refuse to work under *him*.'

'But I don't even know the man,' Laura protested.

'You're not missing much, whereas Dr Ferris, our paediatrician, is an absolute sweetie. Saunders retires in March, don't you, Saunders? Most of us would give our right arms to have the children's ward fall into our laps.'

'Then what use would you be in any ward?' Laura joked. 'Of course children's wards are attractive, but I

14

hope I don't sound pompous when I say that one wouldn't be truly happy if one could pick and choose, or had just what one liked in our profession.'

The Sisters weren't summoned on duty by whistle, but by the dining-room supervisor, who appeared in the doorway saying, 'Eight forty-five, ladies.'

'I'm going to see Matron,' Laura announced.

'Ah, yes. Oh, this is Trevor coming along now.'

Sister Trevor wore the white overall, with navy-blue epaulettes, which betokened the non-resident Sister working in hospital. Martyn made a hasty introduction and hurried off to her geriatric patients.

'I'm on theatre,' announced the newcomer. She was pretty in a Balkan way, with slightly-slanting green eyes and ash-blonde hair, cut very straight and nicely shaped to her small head. 'I suppose you're on your way to see the dragon? Well, I haven't time to natter; it's E.N.T. day and we've got a long list; but if she offers you Orthopaedics, don't take it. O.K.?'

'Why on earth——?' asked Laura, feeling rattled, and not liking Sister Trevor from the outset. She was somehow too white and shining and perfect to be true.

'Well, I can't explain now, but it's obviously important or I wouldn't have mentioned it. We Sisters must stick together in a small hospital. I suppose you agree with that?'

'Well yes, but——'

'So there are other jobs going. Take anything else but——' and away she went tip-tapping down the tiled corridor as though she was a queen and had nodded one of her subjects regally from her sight.

Laura felt like a cat which has been stroked the wrong way. She was a mass of invisible prickles.

Miss Trueblood might have been an incarnation of that first and greatest of all nurses, Florence Nightingale. She was tall and slim without being bony, and her eyes lit up when she spoke of nurses and nursing.

'Actually, I'll be frank with you, Nurse,' she said with a smile that was almost intimate. 'I know Miss Maguire very well. We trained at the Middlesex together.' Laura flushed, because Miss Maguire was the Matron of St Christopher's, her last hospital, who had accepted her resignation with such regret and yet agreed she ought to move on elsewhere. 'She told me you might have difficulty getting reinstated, and I believe you did?'

'Yes, I—yes,' Laura agreed faintly. 'When people heard, they——' and she glanced up helplessly.

'I know. I know.' Miss Trueblood's eyes were warm and sympathetic. 'No matter what the Coroner says, and how extenuating the circumstances are, when one has appeared in a Coroner's court as contributing to someone's death, one might as well buy a little bell and cry "Unclean! Unclean!" It leaves a stigma.'

'Then, Matron, why did you——?' Laura looked up in surprise at the other.

'Because I took Margaret Maguire's word for it that you were a good nurse who had made one mistake in a career of otherwise unparalleled excellence. She assured me you'd be so careful in future you'd be in danger of becoming a prig. Was she right?'

Laura smiled and said, 'Yes, Matron, she was right. I thought of retiring from nursing at first, but then I wanted just another chance to prove myself. I'm not criminally careless by inclination.'

'I'm sure you're not. What happened, exactly?'

'But, Matron, I thought you knew——'

'Of course I know the bald facts,' Miss Trueblood's wave of dismissal accounted for these though she proceeded to enumerate them. 'I know you were acting Sister on an intensive-care ward looking after advanced cardiacs. I know you had one patient on four-hourly stimulant drugs, who missed his injection when due and died because of this. I also know he was a terminal case and could only have lived a week or so at the outside. I also know you were on duty at the time, that he was your responsibility, that the Coroner stated there were extenuating circumstances, that we were all subject to human error when under stress, and that though you would have to live with the memory of the event, everyone else would do well to forget it.'

'Yes, that's about it, Matron,' Laura agreed.

'Right. Now tell me what happened *exactly*.'

Laura could see there was no escape from this soft-voiced, liquid-eyed, determined woman. Hearsay wasn't good enough for her.

'I was on duty, as you know, Matron. What the public didn't know was that I was overdue for annual leave because I was planning to get married. Even this event was postponed indefinitely because of my fiancé's illness. He was apparently very fit, keen on sport, and thought he had strained his back playing rugger. When the trouble persisted, however, I persuaded him to see a specialist, and the awful fact emerged that he was suffering from carcinoma of the spine. I didn't want him to know, but behind my back he insisted, and asked that I shouldn't be told. So there we were playing games, pretending he would get better and planning what we'd do. He was in the hospital where I worked, so I was able to see him a lot without looking too obvious. Matron kept saying that as soon as I could be relieved she'd allow me off duty, because everything was such a terrible strain. I did my work automatically—in fact I could only carry on if I was an automaton—but I kept going. Jim died quite suddenly on the day it—it happened. There was only me and a junior probationer on the ward, and Matron came to tell me in person. She was very kind, but she reminded me that we had all expected it to happen and what a blessing it was if I thought about it. She also said she was getting Nurse Peters out of bed to come and take over if I could just hang on another half hour or so. Well, for half an hour or so I was still an automaton, and efficient, but then I began really to think and to realise I was never going to see Jim again and life loomed at me vast and empty and meaningless. I remember glancing at my watch and it was four o'clock, and I didn't remember giving the two o'clock injections. I looked at the charts and they weren't filled in. I then called Dr Meadows and told him what I had omitted to do and asked him for instructions. Mr Mortlake went into heart-failure almost immediately, and though stimulants were injected and his heart massaged, he—he died within the hour.'

'This conversation is strictly in confidence,' said Matron, 'and so are my comments. You poor girl!' and her hand came out humanly and sympathetically to pat the other's shoulder. As though realising such behaviour was not in keeping between members of the nursing profession while in uniform, she put both her hands on the blotter in front of her, blinked a few times and then asked, 'What happened next, Nurse? You might as well finish it.'

'Well, there was an official hoo-hah, of course, and I was told the Coroner was being informed. I was also relieved of duty until further notice. I remember thinking that in all the awfulness of that day, Matron's decision struck me as particularly awful, as shortage of staff had caused the trouble in the first place. If she could relieve me then, when it had happened, why couldn't she have relieved me earlier? Of course I see now, she couldn't keep me when I had apparently been criminally careless. So there was Jim's funeral and the Coroner's court, and I think you know the outcome of that. Everybody was very kind; the Coroner, the medical staff, Matron and even the man's relatives. Nobody had expected him to be kept alive so long. So it seemed that I got away with my lapse, officially, but Matron made me realise it wouldn't do for me to stay on at St Christopher's. I tried writing off for one or two other jobs, but always that business had to be mentioned, together with the Coroner's remarks, and very gently I was informed that the position had been filled, or something similar. I was thinking I would have to find some other sort of job, in desperation, when

Matron told me to try here, and—and here I am,' Laura finished rather lamely.

'Yes, well,' said Miss Trueblood, 'somebody had to give you a chance to prove your worth sooner or later. I now see there was an emotional cause for your terrible slip—for terrible it was, in the nursing code, as you well know. Like the famous actress, who goes on stage and gives a brilliant comedy performance while her private life is lying in ruins about her, so must the good nurse be a machine of efficiency, comfort and dependability while she is on the wards. Our patients only enter hospital because they trust us implicitly to make their welfare our primary concern. But when the efficient machine is also human, then human error must be allowed for, at least once. I understand your moment of weakness because I, too, have endured such a loss. I was on duty when my only son was killed in a motoring accident three years ago. Ah, yes, I *am* married, though I have been widowed so long not many people know of it, and I am known by my maiden name in the hospital. When the news was broken to me I was doing a ward round, and I found myself insisting on finishing it. I don't think I accounted for a human life, but I cannot remember one patient's name, face or complaint that was thereafter pointed out to me. Like you, I had a sort of blackout, and only in a state of mental and emotional aberration did that dreadful day in my life pass away. But now to business, because you are, after all, here to work, are you not?'

Laura felt she had now been put in her place. Confidences were exchanged and over with.

'One wonders,' Miss Trueblood proceeded, 'if there is anyone else in your life at the moment? A young man, I mean. You're young, very pretty, and it must be nearly a year since your fiancé died.'

'No,' Laura said unequivocally. 'Nobody could take Jim's place. It would be—well—second best, and that wouldn't do for me.'

'One does recover, you know. One doesn't forget, of

19

course, but life has to go on.'

'Still,' Laura said promptly, 'I'll be content with nursing from now on. Where would you like me to start, Matron?'

'Well now, that's up to you, Nurse. I am addressing you as "Nurse" because your decision depends on your status here. Sister Saunders, in the children's ward, is almost due for retirement and could do with experienced assistance now, immediately, as her hearing is rapidly failing. But as we can only have one Sister on a ward you would start there as staff nurse, doing most of Sister's duties as well as your own, with Miss Saunders supervising and simply waiting out her time. Automatically, if satisfactory, you would be promoted Sister of Children when she retires. Alternatively I could offer you a senior position in Outpatients, but I don't like a good nurse wasted there, frankly. It is a necessary job, I know, but actually a married part-timer could do it, and does, at the moment. She is a staff nurse, but I think she deserves promotion. It might encourage her to stay with us as she is West Indian and thinking of going home. Now what I would like you to do, though I won't press the appointment, is to take charge of the orthopaedic ward and be appointed full Sister from the start.'

'Why don't you press the appointment, Matron?' Laura felt she had a right to know.

'Ah, now—' Miss Trueblood's eyes became opaque behind their lens—'I think in current vernacular you have already been "got at", Nurse? All my Sisters have been anti-orthopaedic for some months. I have my own ideas about the ban, though, like the captain of a ship, I must stand aloof from my crew and not listen to gossip. I think, in a nutshell, you will be unpopular with your colleagues if you accept my recommendation, and what form that will take I have no idea. Our senior orthopaedic specialist is a brilliant man, but not the easiest of people to get along with at times. He is inclined to be—er—blunt and not to suffer fools gladly. It sometimes appears that he meets more fools in his day's work than most.' Matron twinkled almost imperceptibly. 'I have not always escaped his tongue, I may add, though I am in a position to tell him a thing or two in return. Now I haven't made the orthopaedic ward sound exactly like Aladdin's Cave, have I? So why should you accept the appointment? I'll tell you. Many othopaedic patients are long-term, especially ours, as we don't accept operation cases. Those are sent to Millerdown, where our Mr Warwick is also employed. I think when you are sentenced to be in bed, maybe in plaster maybe in splints, and perhaps for over a year, that you should be able to think the staff are settled, too, to take an interest not only in your admission but in your progress—or lack of it—and discharged eventually. This necessary feeling of security has lately been lacking, and I am thinking only of the patients when I say this. I have been forced to employ a Sister from a private agency, which is not only expensive but unsatisfactory. Mr Warwick somehow gets rid of them as fast as I procure them, which means the average private nurse lasts less than a month. Sister Lightfoot goes next Wednesday. She has an opportunity of taking a private patient to the Bahamas, so who can blame her?'

'Mr Warwick surely can't be that bad?' asked Laura. 'I mean if one does one's work, and follows instructions——?'

'Mr Warwick has also had an upset personal life,' Matron explained, 'though he'd kill me for mentioning it, no doubt. All I know is that he's been rather difficult lately. I think he minds this internal vendetta, though he'd die rather than appeal to anyone. He's extremely efficient at the job and popular with patients. They don't only admire him, they seem to love him.'

'I'm tempted to take this orthopædic job,' Laura said, 'and not only because of the promotion. I like orthopaedic work especially.'

'Don't give me your answer immediately,' Matron said repressively. 'Think about it. Let me know this time tomorrow. Have a look round today; talk to people; help out if you feel like it. I must mention your—er—history to the medical staff, by the way. You understand that? I'm sure it will make no difference.'

'I hope not,' Laura said from the heart. 'That might give Mr Warwick something to be beastly about.'

'Now, now, Nurse,' Matron hushed her. 'Mr Warwick may be an angry young man, temporarily, and an unhappy one, but he is not unjust. I personally like him tremendously.'

'Well, thanks for explaining everything, Matron,' Laura stood up knowing that she had already taken up a good deal of the other's time. 'I'll give you my answer tomorrow morning.'

'Very good, Nurse. I hope you'll be happy here.'

'Thank you.' Matron nodded and Laura left her presence. Already her mind was made up, but she had to play out the twenty-four hours Matron had allowed her before she could declare her decision.

She felt like a fish out of water wandering from ward to ward, department to department, without belonging anywhere and where everybody was too busy about the morning's business to give much heed to her. In the children's ward Sister Saunders said she hoped Laura would be joining her.

'Oh, I don't think so,' Laura said promptly.

'Outpatients, then?'

'I think Outpatients is well catered for, Sister.'

'Oh, but you wouldn't——? It makes it unpleasant for the rest of us.'

'I don't see why.'

'Well, if you'll excuse me, I'm very busy.'

Apparently the grapevine had been busy, as when Laura went to lunch she found the other Sisters eyeing her coldly. It was Sister Trevor who spoke.

'Bradfield, you can't really mean that you're going to Orthopaedics after what I told you?'

Again Laura felt a bridling against this young woman.

She almost sensed her hair rising on her head.

'I don't think you really told me anything, Sister, and I'm not used to being told to do this or that without good reason.'

Trevor's green eyes narrowed.

'All right, then, I'll give you a jolly good reason. I suppose you've heard of *esprit de corps* among nurses; loyalty to one's fellows and all that? I mean we *have* to stick together. Sister Yorke was a friend of ours, as well as a colleague, and she married Jon Warwick, God rest her soul! Not only did he get her pregnant but he scarcely ever stayed at home with her. He practically lived at the hospital, even sometimes asking for a bed to stay the night. He made poor Jean terribly unhappy; I know, because she told me so. She said he hated the idea of the child and blamed her for it. Some men, I ask you! Anyway, you'd have thought he'd have cared when Jean was brought in prematurely in labour. Not he. He had an emergency at Millerdown. Jean gave birth to a premature boy, and he still didn't come near. Next day Jean had a haemorrhage and I think Dr Watkyn, our R.M.O., brought Jon here by force, so he was with Jean when she died. Yes, she died,' Trevor told Laura bitterly, 'having a child, which had apparently offended him. He never even asked to see it. The midwives kept it alive and Dr Falconer was a saint. He has left the hospital now, but he did more for poor Jean in her hour of need than that rotter, her own husband, did. Even when the baby was christened, when it was touch and go with him, he told the midwives, "Oh, call him what you like. What's in a name?" Can you imagine such callous behaviour? So the baby was named Simon, after the ward he was born in, and he lived and thrived, and you know what his fond father did? He shoved him off with foster-parents. You'd have thought he'd have taken his son home and employed a nanny. Well, wouldn't you? He's not a poor man. So we all got together and decided to boycott the orthopaedic ward so long as Jon Warwick was in charge.

He hasn't known where he's been since, and that—so far as we're concerned—is that. We wouldn't welcome any blacklegs in *our* hospital, and I hope you now see reason.'

Laura looked rather miserably down at the boiled cod and mashed potato on her plate.

'It seems you've only heard the wife's side,' she told the table at large. 'Maybe the marriage didn't work and *he* was unhappy.'

Trevor's eyes flashed angrily.

'We're doing our best to see he is now,' she said.

'But I *didn't* know Sister Yorke; I wasn't working here at the time, and I think I can see things more dispassionately. Why should he have been here awaiting the birth of the child if he could be of more use elsewhere? I don't suppose anybody expected the haemorrhage or her death. Why should the R.M.O. have to drag him here? I'd rather believe he went to warn him, gently, that complications had arisen and offered to drive him over. I think you're seeing things rather over-emotionally, if you don't mind my saying so.'

'Well, we do!' Trevor snapped. 'You can't come here and boss us around, you know.'

'I don't want to,' Laura said, astounded. 'On the other hand *you* can't choose my enemies for me or ask me to carry on a vendetta which I think affects the efficiency of this hospital.'

'Oh, surely you don't really think——?' Sister Martyn asked worriedly.

'Of course not!' Trevor answered sharply. 'I knew Bradfield was a mischief-maker the first time I set eyes on her. Well, let her go to Orthopaedics and be kicked in the teeth by that devil for her pains. But don't let her think she has any friends here—among us. If you have anything so say to me in future, or any of us, say it through a third party. You can't run with the hare and hunt with the hounds here. From now on you're in Coventry.'

'It seems more like an infant school to me,' Laura retorted, stung to anger at last. 'Well, at least I won't miss

24

what I've never had,' and she rose from the table and walked out of the room without a backward glance.

The next morning Laura told Matron she had decided to accept the orthopaedic appointment, and Miss Trueblood didn't ask why she was looking so pale and tense.

Already Laura had been shunned by her colleagues at the breakfast table and Trevor had apparently come in early to see that they did it. It was the first time in her life that she had been made to feel invisible, and it was an extremely uncomfortable experience.

'You had better take over from Sister Lightfoot,' Matron went on, 'as this is her last day with us. She'll introduce you to the patients and staff. I don't know whether Mr Warwick's coming in today or not, as I believe he's been a bit under the weather. But if he is we'll have our little ceremony.'

'Ceremony, Matron?' asked Laura.

'Well, yes. We're only a small hospital, but we appoint our Sisters officially. I can lend you a navy-blue dress, but we present you with a silver buckle. It's rather nice usually.'

But Laura's appointment was not exactly usual, as she discovered to her cost. She rather enjoyed her morning on her new ward, meeting a couple of youngsters supine on spinal beds, searching her face bending over them as if for reassurance that she cared, and various people of both sexes with limbs locked and twisted in arthritis, and a young man who reminded her of Jim, in that a life of sporting activity had suddenly been curtailed when an infection attacked and slowly consumed one knee-joint; he would henceforward be a cripple. In all this she temporarily forgot that another ordeal faced her at lunchtime. The silent Sisters cut her as dead as at breakfast while chatting animatedly among themselves.

When towards the end of the meal Matron and two members of the medical staff entered the dining-room, there was a hush of expectation.

'We are here to appoint a new Sister to our ranks,' Miss Trueblood declared. 'Will Sister Bradfield please come forward?'

As Laura rose a slow hand-clapping accompanied her from the Sister's table. Her cheeks flamed and she saw that some of the staff nurses joined in the demonstration. She looked towards Miss Trueblood who was smiling encouragingly, however; almost admiringly.

Laura advanced to that terrible din, head held high but feeling by no means happy. She did not look up at the man who spoke to her and offered her a silver-buckled belt, telling her he hoped it fitted. She proved it putting it on there and then.

'Well, at least this time it was different,' the masculine voice went on jokingly. 'You've obviously raised the devil, Sister, so now there remains the deep blue sea.'

At last Laura looked up into the very blue orbs of the man she had helped on the cliff-top. So this was the redoubtable Mr Warwick, was it?

'You!' her lips framed, through the din of the slow hand-clapping and some cheering from fairer-minded members of the staff.

'Yes, me!' she heard him reply quite distinctly. 'Now that you've got your bauble, why don't you, too, get lost?'

Anger burned in a white heat behind her eyes. She had suffered this terrible humiliation from her fellows only to find the one man in the world she could find it so easy to hate leering down at her. At that moment she felt convinced that all she had heard about him must so obviously be true, and that, in her innocence, she had taken the wrong side.

CHAPTER TWO

By the following morning Laura was beginning to know her patients as individuals rather than as case-histories, which she had dutifully read up; also she was beginning to find the true worth of her supporting staff. After that rather terrible initiation of yesterday, and finding out her new boss was a man she would have preferred never to meet again in her life, she had returned to her ward to find her rather dour staff nurse, whose name was Pringle, looking even more tight-lipped and unapproachable than ever.

Laura had concluded that the staff nurse was on the side of the Sisters, by her attitude, in that though they had occasionally to speak and discuss their patients, Pringle said only what was necessary and then waited obviously to be dismissed. She was, however, a good and thorough worker, and as long as this was so Laura was quite prepared to put up with the cool atmosphere.

On this morning, however, while Laura was sorting the mail, Nurse Pringle knocked on the door marked 'Sister' and entered, as usual standing with her hands clasped behind her. Laura looked up.

'Yes, Staff Nurse?' she inquired.

Pringle was plain as a currant bun, but as neat and clean as a new pin. Her shoes were square-toed, unfashionable and looked comfortable. They enabled her to move down the ward like an athlete.

'If you'll excuse me, Sister, I would like a word. . .'

'Certainly, Staff Nurse.'

'I was in early and we've got on very well. I've started Wilkie and Rodriguez on pressure points and I'll be doing my dressing-round next. . .'

Laura waited expectantly for some favour to be asked. Pringle had never said so much previously or looked so flushed and embarrassed. Maybe she was going to ask to be transferred. Laura swallowed but never blinked.

'I just wanted to say, Sister, if you'll excuse me, that I didn't expect to see you on duty this morning. I—I think it was awful them carrying on the way they did yesterday, and nobody would've blamed you if you'd cut and run.'

Laura managed a tight little smile.

'I'm not one who cuts and runs to order, Staff Nurse,' she said wryly. 'It never occurred to me not to come on duty.'

'Well, I had to speak. I hope you don't mind. I mean some of our lot joined in and I was ashamed of them. I wanted you to know *I* didn't.'

'Thank you, Staff Nurse.'

'And I won't. I told them a thing or two last night. Well——' she hesitated and one hand actually escaped and came into view fiddling with the immaculate apron.

Laura smiled and her eyes were soft. 'Thank you for telling me, Staff Nurse,' she said, which was the furthest she could unbend from the loneliness of her new rank. 'Better get on with the dressing-round now. I'll take the mail.'

She felt much happier to know she had one ally on the ward, as she set forth to have a word with each of her patients and give them their mail. The third-year nurse, Wilkie, was inclined to be something of a wag—whoever was working with her was usually in stitches—but as Laura passed her and Nurse Rodriguez, a Gibraltarian, Nurse Wilkie said loudly and brightly, 'Good morning, Sister.'

'Good morning, Nurses,' Laura returned, wondering if the girl was about to follow up her greeting with a jeer under her breath. She heard what followed her passing quite clearly, however.

'Rub there, Rodriguez. Don't take the skin off, you

28

heavy-handed clot! I think she's going to be O.K., don't you?'

'Mrs Sweeny?' asked Rodriguez, smiling at their patient. 'Of course she be O.K.'

'*Sister*, you little moron. I mean she's got pluck, you must admit. That Trevor can be a devil. I was under her on theatres last year, so I *know*. When she says jump, the others jump, but ours didn't, and that takes pluck.'

'Please, what is pluck?'

'Oh, lord! This blooming league of nations I work in! Nobody understands the Queen's good English any more. And rub, you twerp! All you're doing is holding the talcum.'

'Nurses,' Laura said gently, which was her way of saying she could hear, 'do talk a little less and try and get finished before the round.' She contrived to give Wilkie a little smile and moved on to the far end of the ward where the chronic arthritics lay, day in, day out, some with hands and feet distorted and terribly twisted.

'Mrs Kershaw, a letter for you. Can you manage to open it yourself?'

'No, Sister. Can—can you do it?'

'Certainly. Here, let me put your glasses on and then you can read it yourself while I hold it.'

'You're—not too busy, Sister?'

'Now, how could I be too busy but with my patients, eh, Mrs Kershaw?'

The other relaxed and then read avidly.

'It's from my Mary, in Canada, Sister. She's 'ad another baby, a boy. She wishes I could see 'im. They're calling 'im Robert after Dad.'

'How nice!' said Laura, as a tear squeezed out of the woman's eye. 'It's such a good, solid name, too. It won't date. I feel a bit sorry for the Tarquins and Damians as they grow up into normal little ruffians.' She wiped the tears away with a tissue.

'Dad died last year,' sniffed the woman.

'I'm sorry. Mary's obviously trying to make it up to

you in the only way she knows.'

'Yes, I must think of that. Would you turn over, now, Sister? Oh, Mary says they might get over next year when Neil gets his bonus. How exciting! June, she says.'

'Then we'll have to try to get you on your feet somehow,' Laura decided. Mrs Kershaw was being built up in health for an operation to break the bones in her hands and feet and reset them.

'Will you be here long, Sister?' Mrs Kershaw asked.

'I hope so. I want to see some improvement in you while I'm here.'

'They come and they go, you know, the Sisters. Miss Benson and me were saying, we're too much trouble for you.'

'Rubbish! We'll have time to become friends. Think of it like that.'

A word or two here, a little assistance there, hearing out the grousers and persuading the uncomplaining to complain if there was anything wrong, Laura eventually arrived at the spinal bed of the youngest member of the ward, thirteen-year-old Amanda Wade, whose last memory of normality had been of feeling her pony rise under her at the goad of her heels to take the five-barred gate at the local junior gymkhana. Alas for Amanada that Pierrot had stumbled on landing and thrown her, then rolled on her. Before nightfall Amanda had been admitted to Millerdown for several urgent operations, including one for a perforated lung. The pony, unhurt but shaken, had been killed humanely on the orders of the father who could demonstrate his anger and panic in no other way. If his daughter survived the crushing and the haemorrhage there would still be the fractured spine to contend with. The accident had happened a year ago and now Amanda would live, if such existence could be called living. She was a moaning, apparently unattractive girl with lank, brown hair and grey eyes.

'Hello, Amanda!' greeted Laura. 'Had a good night?'

'No. Everything hurts and they won't give me my injections any more.'

'Oh, dear! Tell me where it hurts.'

'My legs and my back. I get awful pains. I thought paralysed people felt nothing. It doesn't seem fair.'

'No, it doesn't. But think of it this way. Your nerves are still trying. As long as they try you make up your mind to bear and to help them. I can give you tablets for the pain, but the injections had to be stopped. Where's your reading stand?'

'The cleaner never brought it back.'

'Then you should have shouted for it. When you can't get things for yourself we're all here to do things for you. Nurse Manning—' Laura called to the pretty doll-like girl who was the ward's junior student nurse—'please see that Amanda has her reading stand and any books or papers to hand she wants.'

'Yes, Sister.'

Laura went off to the men's ward, of which she also had nominal charge, but was run very efficiently by Staff Nurse O'Connell, a big Irish girl who had been on an orthopaedic ward previously. Her assistants were Nurse Golightly, known by her companions as the "deb's delight" owing to her very plummy accent, and Nurse Addams, a Jamaican, with Nurse Penn as junior. After a quick word all round Laura again lingered near the spinal bed where sixteen-year-old Tony Devon lay, smiling and cheerful, though he was strapped down, unable to move even where he could with his spine fractured in two places. He couldn't even read, being unable to turn the pages of a book with his arms immobilised and not being allowed the use of the mouth-functioned apparatus, as his head and neck were in a retaining harness.

'Hello, beautiful!' he said cheekily as Laura's head bent over him. 'How long are *you* here for? A week?'

'A bit longer than that, I hope. Long enough to see you in a different position from that, I can tell you.'

'Go on! I didn't think anybody would stay on this ward as long as that. You're kidding!'

'No, I'm not kidding. Now, are you sore anywhere? I'll be back to give you a rub after the round.'

'Me—me bottom's a bit raw,' he said in boyish embarrassment, 'but apart from that I'm fine. It—it's nice to know somebody's staying at last in this dump.'

It was because of the likes of Tony and Amanda, Jim Potts with the infective arthritic knee and Mrs Kershaw with her distorted rheumatoid limbs that she was glad she had defied the other Sisters and come here to serve where, surely, she was most needed.

The patients were enjoying the mid-morning drinks of either Bovril or Horlick's, and Laura was filling in the charts from the drug register when her office door opened without ceremony and Jon Warwick stood revealed with a dark cowlick of hair hanging over a very blue eye.

'Sister,' he said without preamble, 'I'm starting my round now,' and away he went.

'Mr Warwick,' she called out in annoyance, and in the corridor he was awaiting her looking quizzical, 'it wants half an hour to the round and the patients are having drinks. The—the ward isn't ready,' she finished lamely, for her training had taught her that before a doctor's or Matron's round all trivia, such as dirty dishes, must be removed from patients' lockers and all must look tidy and neat and uncluttered.

'Let them carry on drinking,' he said with a shrug. 'They're more relaxed over a cuppa. I fit my round in when I can,' he said coldly, 'and it's right now. Any more objections?'

'Of course I have objections, sir,' her voice quivered. 'The charts aren't ready. I was doing them.'

'Then shove 'em on a trolley and bring 'em along as they are, Sister. Only stop blethering.'

He went through the open doors into the ward leaving her seething with anger. It was only when she remembered that this must be the way all the other Sisters on his wards had been treated recently that she controlled herself and collected the charts and notes together with a ball-point pen. Matron had called him 'A difficult and outspoken young man who didn't suffer fools gladly,' and it *was* foolish to let someone else make one feel so furious. Looking cool and efficient, Laura joined the frowning Mr Warwick as he sat casually on Mrs Kershaw's bed.

'You took your time, Sister,' he observed pleasantly as Laura handed him the woman's chart.

'Oh, come, sir,' she answered in the same mock-teasing voice, 'would you have me scurry like a hen and drop everything?'

Something resembling a smile passed over the blue eyes, but the granite of the mouth never softened.

'This girl tells me she may have visitors next June,' he then observed, while the elderly woman eyed him adoringly. 'We've got to get her out of bed before then and up on her feet. How's her general health?'

'You feel quite fit on the whole, don't you, Mrs Kershaw?'

'Yes, I——'

'I asked you, not the patient,' Jon said curtly, and smiled at the woman while Laura seethed afresh and seemed to be swallowing gall. 'This girl would jump on to the operating table at Millerdown tomorrow, if I'd let her. But what I want to know is if she would heal and so forth?'

'I'm not a physician, Mr Warwick.'

'No. Thank God for that, at least. I thought you might have a little of what is called woman's intuition. Some dedicated nurses do have that inexplicable commodity, I find.'

'Well, mine wouldn't work after only twenty-four hours even if I had it, sir. You'll have to give me more time to prove my supernatural powers *and* my dedication.'

Mrs Kershaw was looking from one to another of the combatants, sensing the contest of wills but wondering how she would fare in the outcome of it.

'Am I ready for the operation, then, Doctor?' she asked.

33

'I'm going to leave you in Sister's hands for a week or two before we decide that, my dear. After all, she's new, and she'll have a bit of clean-sweeping to do. But when she's settled down we'll see if she thinks you'll do.'

Being spoken of as though she wasn't present made Laura grow pale with anger. At the next bed she positively slammed the chart on its backboard into his hands and he promptly dropped it.

'Sister!' he said sharply, and she noticed the wrist in a leather support which had held a boy from his death for goodness knew how long. She was ashamed of her petulance and reached down for the chart, saying hastily before she could change her mind, 'I'm sorry, sir.'

The round progressed and she had to admit he seemed to get on well with patients, could spare a little time and a word of encouragement for those lying in their plaster jackets, or in complicated splints or with fractures which wouldn't knit because of old age or general physical debility. He was very sweet with Amanda who tried to wheedle him into allowing her to have injected pain-killers once again.

'What pain have *you* got, you rascal?' he teased.

'I hurt all over. Honestly, Doctor. I cried all night with my back.'

'Rubbish!' he said sweetly. 'You know I'm waiting for you to get up on your feet and be my best girl at the hospital hop. Don't keep me waiting too long or I might be tempted to ask Sister here.'

'I already have a date, whenever that might be,' Laura chipped in. 'He's all yours, Amanda.'

The round over, new instructions scribbled in her notebook, Laura relievedly re-entered her office to carry on with her interrupted desk work.

'Well?' came from behind her. 'Do your stuff, Sister, I haven't all day.'

'I really thought I'd done my stuff already, sir,' she said quite nastily, 'at great inconvenience. What now?'

34

'Don't I get a cuppa?' Jon Warwick demanded. 'In all the stories about doctors and nurses the heroine's forever putting the kettle on.'

'I'm no heroine, sir, but I'll certainly make you refreshment. Do you prefer tea or coffee?'

'Coffee, black, and two lumps, please. I can't remember whether I had breakfast. I was supervising an op. at five a.m.'

She plugged her own personal kettle into the socket and opened her cupboard where she kept her private rations for special visitors and three attractive china cups and saucers left over from her favourite tea-set at home in Oxfordshire. She wondered who looked after him and if his ill-humour towards senior women staff was founded on unfortunate relationships or indigestion. She handed him a cup of steaming hot coffee and offered him both tiny ham sandwiches and assorted biscuits. The sandwiches she had made herself in her room in case she felt she couldn't bear the dining-room and being cut dead by her fellows.

'I say, these are good,' Jon Warwick said appreciatively, coming back for more sandwiches. 'They couldn't have been meant for me, so—I say, Sister—' his eyes gleamed mischievously—'you must have a follower!'

'No,' she said, apparently glibly, 'and if I did I would expect him to be hungry only for me.'

She met his eyes while feeling the colour mounting her neck, and his were smiling appreciatively. Her own lips trembled to smile but never quite made it.

'Aren't you having a cup?'

'No, not just yet. But while you have a moment could we discuss Mandy Wade? I think she does have quite a lot of pain. Panadol doesn't seem to help much and Night Sister reported she was wakeful and weepy most of the night.'

He proceeded to tell her of several other pain-killers she might try.

'But I'm not really worried about our young friend

35

any more,' he said. 'She has healed very satisfactorily. She has to suffer a good deal of pain, unfortunately, if she's ever to walk again.'

'She's not to be paraplegic, then?'

'Not necessarily. She was borderline at one time, but there's now no clinical reason why she shouldn't be fully rehabilitated. I only say she's sound clinically, mind. Mentally she's as flat on her back as ever she was. Instead of bullying me,' he continued conversationally, 'give young Amanda hell. Make her good and mad, misunderstood and badly done by. Let her weep and simply hand her a tissue. The physiotherapist will do her own physical urging, but until there's a sharp mental stimulus she's like a car without an engine. Now young Tony—' he added—'may not make his next birthday. Baby him as much as you like, but he won't ask for it. He's got the guts every soldier on a battlefield wished he had.'

'I didn't gather from his notes it was so serious.'

'I'll let you read my private notes on him if you stay. They have been known to read their notes, you know, or relatives will sneak a look and give the game away. I never burden anybody with depressing knowledge unless they have to know. I'm sure Tony's widowed mother would rather have her hopes. She has to work for her living. Well—' he said, suddenly jumping up and making for the door—'we can't all take our ease by the hour. See you, Sister.'

'When will I see you again, sir?' she asked, and added as he looked coy, 'I would like to be prepared next time.'

'Oh, I thought you were asking for a first date.' As she sighed in exasperation he said, 'We can say about ten on Friday, if you like, but it could be half-past and I might even make it by nine-thirty. One the whole it's best to be prepared and expect me when I turn up. I'm a very busy man.' He went out and returned to add, 'Also very easy-going.' He disappeared a second time and came back again. 'They can be doing absolutely anything when I come bar sitting on their bed-pans, and I won't be put out.'

'I will,' Laura leapt up to say sharply. 'This morning has been an absolute shambles and I won't have another one like it.'

'Or else you'll leave us?' he smiled.

'No, you must organise yourself better, sir. Try to think, just for once, that there's room for improvement in you.'

'There *is*?' he asked in annoyed surprise. 'And I thought I was such a wonderful fellow!'

Laura wondered how she had stuck it out for two whole weeks, what with one thing and another. Her colleagues, now, were not only content to ignore her when she met up with them in the dining-room, but talked across her, and, sometimes, about her in her hearing. Once she had flared, 'Can't you shut up and let me get my meal in peace?' But this only brought a grimace from Sister Trevor and an apparently innocent inquiry, 'Did somebody speak, or have we got mice?' and as one or two tittered, Laura decided never to let anybody again imagine that she either heard, or cared, what was said.

The patients, of course, grew to like and have confidence in her, apart from young Amanda, who thought Sister 'had it in' for her and was over-harsh. It hurt Laura physically to see the girl's face drawn with pain as her muscles contracted involuntarily and have to say, shortly, 'You'll just have to do your exercises and put up with it. Don't be a softie.' Mandy's eyes would fill and spill over.

'Sister doesn't like me,' she told the staff nurse. 'She says it's my own fault I'm not walking again. She says I like hogging attention and don't try. But I do try, don't I? It just hurts so much.'

Staff Nurse Pringle would say pacifically, 'She knows more about spinal cases than I do. You must listen to Sister. Even I have to do what she says. That's why she's a Sister.'

'Well, I *hate* her, so there! I hope she doesn't stay long.'

Also Laura had to conclude that Mr Warwick was a difficult man to work under; not thoughtful of staff whom he seemed to think of as sacrifical lambs to the needs of the patients. When he was having a bad day he could be acidly sarcastic, and often had the tenderer-hearted of the junior staff in floods of tears. Nurse Manning, in her first year as a student, had more beauty than brains, or so it always seemed when Jon Warwick was in the vicinity. She would stop and gape, invariably looking like a terrified blue-eyed rabbit before the menace of a snake, and for the duration of his round would be peculiarly accident-prone, dropping and breaking glasses and cups or upsetting bowls from bed-baths at the surgeon's feet, once over his shoes. Laura would try to hustle the juniors from the ward before his advent, but as he still arrived unpredictably, at his own convenience, more often than not everybody was busily occupied with the demands of the routine and in trying to rush the trouble was caused.

'I must ask you, sir,' Laura said, sharply, one day as she gave him his coffee after the round, 'not to be so harsh on Nurse Manning. It's difficult enough getting young girls into nursing. They could earn more than twice their salary in any shop or office and work fewer hours.'

'Nurse Manning is the one who looks like a doll?'

'Yes.'

'And behaves like a blithering idiot?'

'Yes. But——'

'Ah, so you agree she *is* a bit dim?'

'She's got the necessary "O" levels.'

'There's no "O" level in nursing, Sister. You're either a nurse or you're not. That girl is not. Better to find it out before she kills somebody.'

He was about to leave the office when he turned and regarded her biting her lip, her colour rather high.

'I'm sorry, Sister. That was clumsy of me.'

'That's all right, sir.'

'No, it isn't. I usually know exactly what I'm saying even when it's not very pleasant to hear. For once I spoke without thinking and I do apologise. Also I'll try not to be harsh on our dolly girl. You can probably lick her into some sort of shape if she sticks it.'

'Thank you, sir.'

She thought it was rather big of him to have apologised like that, though she naturally wondered what he had thought when he had first been told of her 'crime'. She felt rather more kindly about him until he arrived for the round one day two hours late. Having concluded that he didn't intend coming in until afternoon she had started to serve the dinners.

'You really are impossible, sir,' was torn from her, as she surrendered her place at the serving trolley to Pringle and went to collect the charts.

'Let them feed,' he said, settling down in her chair at her desk. 'I'm in no hurry.'

'Are—are you sure?' she asked uncertainly.

'Sure I'm sure. Carry on.'

She proceeded to carry on though she was extremely conscious of the waiting figure in the office. After the main course she went to look and he was fast asleep, his long legs lying across the desk. After that she gave the patients their dessert, looked at the sleeper again and proceeded to serve the coffee.

'Oh, Staff Nurse,' she said at last, 'do you know what Mr Warwick does on Wednesday afternoons? He's fast asleep, you see, in my office.'

'I believe it's his p.p. day, Sister. Maybe he hasn't many appointments. But you ought to wake him and ask, I suppose.'

'Would you—er—wake him up, Staff?'

'I—I would rather not, Sister. But it's up to you——'

'I'll do it myself, Staff. I only hope he doesn't wake up in a rage. I'll take him a cup of coffee.'

She set down the cup and gently shook his shoulder, getting a grunt in reply.

'Mr Warwick, sir——?' she urged in his ear.

'Mmmmm?' he murmured, seized her hand and held it cupped against his cheek in sleepy contentment. She pulled her hand away sharply and the blue eyes shot open, became aware and looked round in realisation and disappointment.

'Now that was some dream!' he commented. 'What time is it, Sister?'

'After one, sir. The patients are ready if you are.'

'Oh, yes. Patients. Actually I'm not doing a full round. I'm going home to bed. Come with me, Sister?'

'Sir?' she asked, startled.

He began to laugh in genuine amusement. 'To see our patients,' he chuckled. 'I must say you've gone quite pale. Forgive the ambiguity. It was quite unintentional. Actually I do not play around with nurses nowadays. The uniform, to me, is not attractive.'

'I'm sure your sentiments are reciprocated, sir,' she told him quickly. 'All medical staff are not, contrary to their belief, the answer to every maiden's prayer.'

He turned to regard her. His eyes were coldly blue while her own were like roasted chestnuts, staring him out.

'Now why do we both enjoy our little exchanges so much?' he asked, to her surprise. 'It's almost as stimulating when we dislike intensely as when we love.'

'But I don't dislike you intensely, sir. I hardly know you. I find you extremely irritating and provocative, but if you are hoping by your behaviour to render me an adversary then you'll be disappointed.'

'I must say I find you have certain failings, too, Sister. Your sharp rejoinders occasionally savour of impertinence and the ricochet comes back often before the bullet is fired. But I'll go home and look in my mirror if you will do the same. If our faults and failings are so obvious to other people we may even glimpse a flaw in ourselves.'

He sailed on then and in that moment she certainly didn't dislike him. She positively hated the creature.

It was not a happy appointment at Thornsea Cottage Hospital, she told herself as she wandered along the cliffs on her day off. She had never in her nursing life known ostracism before, it really hurt. The Sisters of any hospital form an esoteric little group in which are bound their friendships and, occasionally, their animosities. They are subject to Matron and her immediate assistants; they cannot make chums of those lower in order than themselves. Though Laura knew her two staff nurses were loyal to her, and obviously liked to feel settled under someone they could depend on at long last, they had their own personal friends—and some enemies—among others of their own rank. Working hours were now the happiest in her days, with the shadow of the consultant always threatening the even tenor even of these, but though she had always enjoyed her lonely periods of exercise, there had always been friends back at the hospital waiting to rag her about them, or discuss the latest news from the grapevine or speculate on rumours of staff indiscretions. Now there was only work and then her own company, unrelieved by gossip or friendly overtures from her own kind. Sister Mahmoud, a very pretty Pakistani girl, once addressed her as they passed in a corridor.

'I say, Sister, I have just found out what sending to Coventry means. How interesting it all is, your English idiom! I really thought you would have to go to work in the car factories and so on. When you are still here I ask and find out——'

Laura was smiling when Trevor came along, an ice-princess, her white-blonde head held high.

'Mahmoud, you're *not* talking to the blackleg, are you?'

'Well, I—it's all so interesting. Is that more idiom, the blackleg?'

'Now look, Mahmoud, I thought I'd made it all very clear to you. If you talk to her again, you, too, are in Coventry.'

'Oh, Sister! Please—I'm sorry, I'm sorry,' she tried to convey to Laura, who turned away with dignity without

41

saying a word. Let them play their childish games. She didn't care. She just *didn't* care. But she scarcely recognised Jon Warwick for the tears in her eyes as he came along at that moment. Her 'Good morning, sir,' was decidedly throaty and made him feel uncomfortable, accompanied as it was by the swimming eyes. Usually she had a brisk, brittle voice she reserved especially for him. When he came upon her unawares he noticed the change in her, the armour under the neat dark print dress, the armament cocked and ready for him. He had her back in form before the end of the round, but he gave her half an hour to recover from whatever it was had beset her.

The physiotherapist was buckling Amanda's stick-like legs into calipers, and the girl was taking quite an interest in this operation until she saw the navy-blue dress in her orbit, and then she whined anew.

'I don't feel well. I'm going to faint.'

'Oh, come, Amanda!' Laura said sharply. 'You've been sitting up in a chair for two weeks now. What's suddenly making you faint? You can't admit, can you, that you're a whole lot better? What are you afraid of? That all your school friends will have left you miles behind in everything? Get a grip on yourself and go after them.'

'I tell you I feel sick,' Amanda stated flatly. 'I can't walk. I don't know why anybody's bothering.'

'It's not so long since you couldn't sit up. Do you remember? Frankly I don't know why we bother.'

Laura passed on and the girl's eyes smouldered.

'Oh, I do *hate* her! She's horrible to me. I'll bet she doesn't know I nearly died when they brought me into hospital at first. Everybody at Millerdown was so lovely and kind. I wish I was back there.'

Sister Trevor had come into the ward while Amanda was speaking, in search of the physiotherapist.

'Hello, Janet. We've got a tracheotomy in Ward Three we'd like you to visit. He's a bit nervous and needs reassuring. Surely you don't mean you'd really like to be back at Millerdown, poppet? You're practically up on your feet again.'

Janet Marsh smiled.

'We're having a hate Sister complex at the moment.'

'Oh? Why?'

'Because she hates me,' Mandy sulked, picking at her fingernails.

'A bit of cruel-to-be-kind,' Janet explained, to put Trevor wise.

'Oh.' Sister Trevor didn't realise she had stored the information away like a squirrel stores nuts. She knew, having worked on so many wards, how patients reacted to sympathy. Some battened on it until they couldn't do without it, while others resented their helplessness so much they fought against it and wwere more likely to win in the race to regain their health.

'I'll come and see you again, pet,' Trevor told Mandy, aware of the other's admiration of her physical perfections, and vanity being her own personal weakness. 'You can tell your troubles to me.'

After another week Amanda was making good progress inside the walking frame in the gym. Her weight was mainly on her arms grasping the rail, but she looked positively triumphant as she dragged one metal-supported limb forward followed by the other, and again, and again.

'I did it!' she told Janet Marsh. 'Why am I sweating?'

'Because you've been working hard. I'm very pleased with you. Mr Warwick will be pleased with you and so will Sister.'

'Oh, I don't care about *her*,' said the ingrate. 'That boy in the men's ward is her favourite. She's always popping off to see him.'

This was true, for since Jon Warwick's rather grim prognosis Laura had tried to make the boy as happy and comfortable as possible. He was her special patient, and she did almost everything for him herself. Not because O'Connell couldn't but because the staff nurse was much too busy to stop and linger over Tony very long. One had to linger over him because his nether region was completely paralysed and he did not always know when he was sore. Lately the question of bed-soreness was becoming rather desperate and Tony was quite poorly, though his poor, pale face would light up for Laura and he'd say, unfailingly, 'Hello, beautiful!'

A messenger came to Laura in her office asking if she could spare a few minutes to see Tony.

'Certainly. I'll come at once.'

But outside the ward a relative of Mrs Kershaw's was asking for news.

'When's her op, Sister? Is she up to it? Will she be able to walk? Use her hands?'

Having answered as well as she could, she then continued into the men's ward. Tony's bed was the first on the right, where it was easier for everyone to keep an eye on him.

'Tony?' she asked softly, and with a warning dip of her heart noticed the open eyes were sightless upon her own.

'Nurse,' she called to the junior, 'please call Staff, will you?'

'Please, Sister, she's gone to dinner.'

'Then whoever is senior.' Laura drew the curtains about the spinal bed and felt for Tony's pulse. It was still and she knew by the feel of the skin, taut over the bones, that Tony was dead. She put her cheek next to the slightly parted lips and no breath damped her. Even while a great sadness welled up inside her—this was the first death on her wards since her arrival—she looked efficient and capable as Nurse Golightly parted the curtains and joined her at the bedside.

'Oh, my aunt!' exclaimed Golightly, in her plummy voice. 'What's happened to Tony?'

'I found him d.i.b. Nurse.' The deb's delight paled. Anybody found dead in bed, without a doctor being called, or relatives, usually meant somebody had slipped up and there would be a row. 'What happened that I was

44

called? Did *you* send for me?'

'No. It was Staff on her way to lunch—er—dinner. She said, "Tell Sister Tony wants her," but I didn't look at him myself. I simply sent Addams for you. I say, Sister, I'm awfully sorry. We were terribly fond of Tony.'

'I think you'd better put a call out for Mr Warwick, or the Registrar, failing him, and Staff had better come along, too. Maybe she knows what Tony wanted. We can't apportion blame at the moment, there's too much to be done.'

Jon Warwick was lunching with Matron and came at once; so did Staff Nurse O'Connell.

'Tony has been a bit restless this morning, sir,' she told the surgeon. 'Sister has been in twice to do his dressings. I was on my way to dinner when he said, "I wonder if Sister would mind coming again, just to hold my hand?" I had a joke with him, asking if Nurse Golightly could hold his hand instead, and he smiled and said he'd rather like a word with his best girl, that being Sister, so I asked Nurse to pass on the message. That was twelve-thirty-five, sir.'

Laura was biting her lip. If only she hadn't been cornered by Mrs Kershaw's sister she might have been with Tony when he died. In those ten minutes a young life had mysteriously slipped away.

'Now I want everybody to listen before we break up,' said Jon Warwick clearly. 'This was bound to happen sooner or later and I don't want it to throw you. He could have sneezed and fractured the damaged spinal cord, or he could have thrombosed just anywhere. He died quickly, though alone, instead of by inches, which was beginning to happen. Personally I'm glad and relieved he's out of it. He was a grand kid and I prefer to think of him kicking a football about somewhere instead of rotting on a spinal bed. But his mother is going to mind, and the Coroner may want to know what happened. Until we get the result of the p.m. we'll keep all this in the family. So everybody had better get back to work.

45

It was agreed that Laura should tell Mrs Devon, who was already a widow and without any other children, and get her permission for the post-mortem without delay.

The woman arrived, collected from her place of work by a police car, and as Laura handed her a cup of tea she said sharply, 'You're going to tell me Tony's dead, aren't you?'

'I'm sorry to say yes, Mrs Devon. We're all most upset. He was a wonderful patient.'

The woman set down her cup and her complexion turned a shade of grey.

'Yes, I'm upset myself. So he's gone, eh? What did he die of? I was at work. I didn't get no message to come.'

'No. Well, he died of his injuries. We won't know how, exactly, until after the post-mortem. We want your permission for that.'

The woman took a sip of the tea and her free hand plucked at her coat. It was obvious that nothing was getting through to her immediately. Nature has her own way of providing shock-absorbers to the human mind. Rather than accept the death of her son, Mrs Devon played around on words.

'Of his injuries, you say, Sister? Why didn't he die of those when it 'appened, then? Why did he lie there, all that time?'

'We have to have the post-mortem, Mrs Devon, and then all your questions will be answered. Do you think you can sign this form for me? Thanks. If it's any comfort to you, Tony didn't suffer. One minute he was his cheery self, having a joke with Nurse, and then it was all over.'

'Nurse was with him when he died, then?'

'Er—no. She wasn't to know he was going to die.'

'Were you with him?'

'No. I——'

'Was anybody with Tony when he died?'

'Not with him. There were two nurses on the ward, but there was no way of telling——'

'You mean he just died, all on his own, strapped down and helpless?'

'I told you it was very quick. Probably like going to sleep.'

'But only probably. We don't know, do we?'

'Come and see him, Mrs Devon. Come on. He was a brave, good boy and it's really a mercy. You must see that. You must remember what he was like running about and playing football, like other boys. . .'

Tony, now technically 'the body', was still on the spinal bed, pulled into an otherwise empty side-ward. No one would be allowed to touch him until the pathologist claimed him for the post-mortem. All that had been done was the closing of the eyes and the binding of the jaw. He looked peaceful, remote and very young.

A dry rack came from the bereaved mother eventually, but there were no tears. Laura sent her home eventually in an ambulance car and informed the nearest clergy-man by phone. She returned to the women's ward feeling bruised and battered, mentally and morally shaken. She would never forgive herself for not answering Tony's last plea immediately by making everyone else wait until she was available. It was no use, she knew, crying over spilt milk, but how differently she would have viewed his dying if she could have granted him the comfort of her presence, his hands gripped firmly in her own.

Though the news of a death is never broadcast to other patients, they seem to have an inbuilt radar in detecting the crises of others, and when the screens go up, and stay up, and are only removed to reveal an empty space or a newly made-up bed, then they draw their own conclu-sions and the grapevine busily spreads the news abroad with a rapidity which is postively frightening.

By tea-time Miss Gates, a spinster with an osteoarth-ritic hip, asked nervously, 'Oh, Sister, I hear that boy died next door. The one who broke his back?'

There was a hush in the beds about, and Laura answered honestly. 'Yes. Well, these things do happen, unfortunately, from time to time.'

47

'They say there was no one there?' pressed Miss Gates.

'Someone is always on the ward,' Laura said quite sharply. 'You should know that.'

She swept on because she had had a bad time and didn't want to add to it. As she passed Amanda's chair the girl whispered to her neighbour, 'I know why she left her last hospital. Somebody died and there was trouble. Maybe she left him to die, too, like Tony. I think she's hard and shouldn't be a nurse.'

Laura had stopped in her tracks and now turned, her eyes hot and her cheeks crimson.

'Who told you that?' she positively blazed, so that Amanda shrank down in her chair and looked petrified. 'Tell me where you got your information,' Laura said more clearly.

'I—don't know. Somebody told me. I can't help hearing things.'

'No. But you can help making malicious allegations, can't you? If you can't say good of anyone, say nothing. That's a good rule to live by.'

She went on her way feeling she would choke if she stayed. How had the past caught up with her, on this of all days? She might have felt better if he had heard the outraged chatter in the ward she had left.

'You didn't ought to have said that about Sister, you ungrateful girl!' said Mrs Kershaw.

'Oh, for goodness' sake, what did I say? I only reported what I heard.'

'I don't care if she killed somebody with her bare hands. She's been a saint on this ward. She buys me tasty snacks with her own money to tempt me, so's I'll get built up. That's how hard she is.'

'Well, you must admit she hasn't done much for me. After all my suffering she tells me I can do no better. That's all I ever get.'

'And isn't it true? You made enough song about sitting up, and now you can walk on crutches. All that's due to Sister. She won't let you rest till you walk out of here as good as new. You should thank her on your knees for rescuing you from that bed where you was content to lie, day in, day out, shouting for your injections.'

Amanda, feeling the bitterness of shame, suddenly began crying. 'I didn't mean it! I'm sorry! It was that Sister with the fair hair told me about the trouble at Sister's last hospital. I didn't make that up. She said she had to leave after a patient died.'

'Well, we can't all live for ever,' said Mrs Kershaw, sturdily. 'She's here, and I for one am glad.'

'So am I,' said Nurse Pringle, breezing down the ward to collect the medicine trolley, 'and now I think we've all had enough excitement for one day. Get ready to tell me whether you've been or not, and get back to normality, eh?'

CHAPTER THREE

THE mutterings at the Sisters' table didn't immediately die down as Laura sat down to dinner at one o'clock the next day. Her thoughts were still on the dead Tony and what was being discovered on the cold slabs of the autopsy room in the hospital basement.

'I really didn't know we were that hard up for nurses,' muttered elderly Sister Saunders, probably more loudly than she intended because of her deafness. 'I think it's disgraceful that people can't put their loved ones in hospital, nowadays, without being sure they're in capable hands.'

'You'd think any decent person wouldn't have the audacity, let alone the confidence, to inflict themselves on sick members of the community again, wouldn't you?' asked Sister Martyn. 'Especially in a position of authority? We all know our own powers, I hope? What I say goes in *my* ward, anyway. I would blame myself for any sloppiness and expect to be blamed. Forgetting that injection on which someone's very life depends is criminal, and I don't care who hears me say it.'

At last Laura knew, with a sinking of her heart, that they were talking about her. She lost interest in the watery Irish stew and dumplings already growing greasy on her plate.

'I am not talking to anybody,' she suddenly said clearly, 'but if I am being talked at I think in all fairness I should be allowed to say something, too. It seems obvious that you have heard a very one-sided version of the business at my last hospital. I——'

'Shame! Shame! Sssss!' Trevor tried to stir up the others and shout her down.

'I hear so much,' said Mahmoud, perhaps ingenuously,

'about English fair play. Is this it? I am interested in all things.'

'I suppose we ought to let her speak,' said West Indian Jepson uneasily. 'There are always two sides to everything.'

'Are you lot softening?' asked Trevor.

'Let her have her say,' granted Martyn. 'We can draw our own conclusions.'

As there was silence, Laura proceeded.'I have the Coroner's report on a patient's death in my possession, as it appeared in a newspaper for all to read. It will be in my office, in my locker, if anybody cares to read it. I give you all permission to open my locker and read it if I'm not available. It doesn't give an emotional account, though emotions were involved. Just the facts and the Coroner's comments, that's all.'

Trevor began to hum 'Hearts and Flowers' and then said, 'I do believe we're being appealed to. Well, I've read the Coroner's report and I've drawn my own conclusions. There was criminal carelessness involved I don't care to have practised in *this* hospital. It begins to look as though it has started.'

The table maid came and said to Laura, 'Sister, you eat less and less each day. Perhaps a little cold chicken? There is some.'

'Chicken to the chicken,' piped up the tormentor, but only she laughed.

'I had a good breakfast,' lied Laura, 'and I enjoyed the soup. Don't worry about me, Betty.'

Jon Warwick was making his way to the Sisters' table—the dining-room was by this time otherwise deserted—and nobody noticed how Trevor's pale countenance flamed and how cold and hard her eyes became.

'Sorry to intrude, ladies,' he said quietly, 'but I just wished to give Sister Bradfield an autopsy report.' Lowering his voice a little, but still speaking so that all could hear, he proceeded, 'The spinal cord had finally severed in the double area of fracture. Death was therefore instantaneous. He couldn't—nobody could have known. As he was having more and more involuntary spasms it could have happened during one of those. I thought you'd like to know.'

'Yes. Thanks. I'm glad Tony couldn't have—have known.' Her voice wobbled with that uncertainty she had felt once before.

'Not a thing,' Jon Warwick emphasised. 'There's no question of an inquest.'

'Lucky for some!' Sister Trevor remarked.

'Oh—and a private word in your ear, Sister.' Jon still addressed Laura pointedly. 'Perhaps we could just step outside?'

'Certainly, sir.'

'Birds of a feather,' Trevor told her colleagues, while Mahmoud looked embarrassed and played with the currant duff and custard in front of her.

Laura looked straight ahead in the corridor outside the dining-room. She could see one of the housemen, wearing a tracksuit, setting off on an hour's jog-trot across the cliffs. A gardener was raking up leaves and a bonfire burned behind the shrubbery. She saw them like characters in a dream through swimming eyes. Tony didn't know—couldn't have known, still rang in her ears. He hadn't sent for her out of any sense of desperation; maybe he just enjoyed her company, the way he imagined she could make him feel more comfortable than anyone else.

'Tell me to mind my own business, Sister,' invited Jon Warwick, 'but are they giving you a very bad time?'

She struggled for the words which seemed to be blocking up her throat. 'I—I don't think they realise how—how much it hurts to be—ostracised,' she managed at length.

'No, I don't suppose they do. Actually they're ostracising me. You realise that, don't you? Because of me—you.'

'They've found out—about what happened at my last hospital.'

'I—I see. That's bad. Look, have dinner with me tonight.'

Her laugh was breathy, faintly hysterical. 'It's—it's not as bad as that,' she tried to joke, and was amazed when tears came. He handed her a hanky without more ado.

'I think it is. You have a right to chuck your hand in if you like, therefore you have a right to know the full facts. We must talk,' he insisted, 'and there's never enough time after rounds. I ought to be at Millerdown now. I'm holding up a conference there. Matron has noticed how thin—er—slim you're becoming, and there wasn't much to start with.'

'I'm a greyhound type,' she managed to smile rather wetly.

'So I'll collect you at eight outside the gates,' he said quietly, 'just so we can chat. O.K.?'

'O.K.,' she agreed. 'I'll go back and have my coffee.' She was obviously collecting herself as for an ordeal.

'Good girl!' he said as he marched off, tall, dark, broad-shouldered, as a good orthopaedic surgeon should be, and busy.

Laura knew it was not a strictly social occasion to which she had been so unexpectedly invited, and so she hesitated to make herself look especially attractive. As she equally rebelled against looking dowdy, she compromised by wearing a plain black cashmere dress and over it a black needlecord coat. The dress had relieving white buttons and lapels, and she was very fond of it, as being smart without appearing fussy. Usually, when not on duty, she let down her hair, but though she would have done so had she been meeting a sweetheart, or even a friend, she decided Jon Warwick was in neither category, but her boss. Thus she dressed it in the usual french pleat she wore under her Sister's cap, and to soften the severity she wore a pair of pearl studs in her ears, but no other jewellery of any kind.

She was prompt at the gates, too, though doubting *he* would be there on time, a busy surgeon's life being extremely unpredictable. The big Jaguar slid up silently within four minutes, however, and remembering the first occasion when she had been in the car she smiled reminiscently. He must have been observant, for he remarked, while apparently watching his driving mirror, 'You seem a bit happier now, Sister.'

'Oh, I am,' she told him. 'I was recalling our first meeting as strangers, on the cliffs, and how you criticised my driving, among other things.'

'I must admit I'm a nervous passenger when the driver's a woman.'

'You had reason to be on that occasion. I had only ever driven a Volkswagen and a small Morris. A Jag felt like a steam engine to steer with an aircraft's tendency to accelerate. I suppose one gets used to it in time.'

'For me it's a practical motor. From my flat I can reach Millerdown in six minutes flat when there's an emergency admission—— Would you like to get a bit more practice in by driving us to the Blue Schooner?'

'Oh, no, thanks!' she laughed. 'I have no ambitions as a driver, and I wouldn't like you to be upset.'

'I've booked a table at the Schooner and informed both hospitals where I can be reached. I don't think we have any crisis cases in the Cottage now that Tony's gone, do we?'

'No.' She was sorry to remember Tony and spared his poor mother a thought. 'The worst about orthopaedic patients is the time they're with us, and the best is that they're usually fit in every other way. Nobody's causing anxiety at the moment, only poor Jim Potts is suffering a lot of pain.'

'That's unfortunately infective arthritis for you. If he's in a better physical shape now, we'll put him in a long plaster on Monday. That should give him ease from those damned starting pains he complains of.'

They pulled up in the car park of the Blue Schooner, a sort of club-restaurant on the outskirts of the town. There was blue neon all round the roof and a spot-lighted picture of an azure ship in a temptestuous navy-blue sea.

'A bit garish,' said Jon, 'but they put on a good meal usually, and one doesn't have to dance. I asked for the table furthest from the band. I hope you don't mind?'

Laura bit back a smile.

'Of course not, sir. We're here, after all, to talk, not dance. Even the food is incidental.'

'Not at all. I can't have my ward Sister fading away for lack of nourishment.' They entered the restaurant. Jon pointed towards a door on which was painted a triangle with legs, or so it seemed. 'You can leave your coat in there and join me in the restaurant. We'll have an aperitif while we're choosing our meal.'

There were about ten couples in the restaurant when she entered, and one party in a corner. From this group came a shrill laugh, and Laura turned to behold Eve Trevor, also apparently dining out, in a green brocade dress, her shoulders bare and very white under the blue, cold lights.

Jon Warwick rose in his place as she approached and continued to stand and stare.

'Your hair——' he said at last.

'What's wrong with it?' She put a hand up wondering if a holding pin had slipped or something.

'You're fair,' he said accusingly. 'Quite blonde.'

'Yes,' she agreed. 'I alwayys have been. Why? Is it a crime?'

'You have brown eyes——'

'I know I inherited my mother's eyes and my father's fairness. It's just the way I am.'

'Yes. I'm sorry. It's those absurd Sisters' hats with the strings. So archaic. I presumed you were brunette.'

'Does it make any difference?' she asked.

'It must—to you. Aren't gentlemen said to prefer blondes?'

'So they say, and marry brunettes. But I'm sure we're not here to discuss my chances of success with the opposite sex.'

'You never know. What will you have?' as a wine waiter hovered over them.

She ordered a Martini and he a gin and tonic. While they sipped they studied the menu and the band began to play a rather dreamy waltz, to which a few couples responded.

'The Chicken Maryland sounds good,' he suggested. 'How about it? All those lovely extras like fried banana and pineapple and broccoli spears cooked in butter. Join me?'

'It sounds delicious,' she agreed. 'I feel quite weak at the thought.'

'And a bottle of Rosengarten '67 to wash it down. Melon to start with?'

She agreed and was actually beginning to enjoy herself a little. It was a long time since she had been out to dine. The last occasion had been a family treat with her parents when she was feeling a bit down, her future uncertain and cold reality dawning upon her that she would never see poor Jim again. It hadn't been a very happy dinner party, though her father had told his wartime jokes and tried to keep good cheer flowing.

They now chatted about inconsequentials until they were half-way through the main course, and then Jon said, apparently casually, 'When your appointment at the Cottage was proposed a few of us were told of the circumstances of your being on the market, so to speak.'

'Oh, yes,' she agreed. 'Matron said you'd have to know.'

'I don't mean about the inquest, etcetera. I mean we were told about your fiancé. That must have been a terrible time for you—everything happening as it did.'

'Yes, it was,' she agreed. 'One doesn't think one will ever recover. But—' and she sighed—'sometimes I have difficult remembering Jim. Isn't that odd?'

'No. I have the same problem. I——'

'Of course,' she said quickly, 'you lost your wife.'

'Yes.' He smiled wryly. 'My difficulty is remembering I

56

ever had one. But I suppose a man finds things that much more tolerable in that love is supposedly such a small part of his existence.'

She wondered if she was meant to respond to this, but didn't. Shrieks of laughter were coming from the party near the band. Eve Trevor's voice could be heard shouting, 'Oo, Laurie, you *are* a scream!'

'Our colleague always manages to do everything she attempts with such panache,' Jon observed wryly.

A waiter was making his way towards the table, and gave a little bow. 'The band will play your request, sir, and here's a message I was asked to deliver.'

'But I didn't——' Jon opened the note and then the band struck up the cheerful strains of 'The Girl I left behind Me.' It was jazzed up so that couples began to quickstep to it. Jon handed the folded slip of paper to Laura, who read, with eyebrows raised, REMEMBER JEAN, before looking back at him.

'Jean was my wife,' he explained, 'and the heavy hand of Sister Trevor is reminding me of it in her own inimitable way. Would you, please, without question, do me the honour of dancing to my supposed request?'

'Well, yes, if you think——'

'I *do* think.'

For a big man he was light on his feet and a good dancer. As a nurse she knew everyone in their profession got a certain amount of practice in the art. There were Christmas dances and Founder's Day hops and celebrations when somebody passed an exam or was promoted. Now they whirled in perfect harmony past the big table where Eve Trevor's eyes goggled and her current drink was suspended in mid-air.

'Good!' he said when it was over, having clapped as hard and long as anybody. 'Now I think you deserve an explanation. Not that you may expect one, but I didn't know Sister Trevor would be here tonight and put on her usual charade which is intended to entertain everybody but me, as you may be sure. You have got yourself rather

57

involved in the game by taking over my wards at the Cottage, no doubt despite her good friendly advice——?'

Laura smiled wryly and nodded. 'I was practically told to accept anything other than orthopaedics, but I'm not easily shoved around. I wanted to know why.'

'And she told you, no doubt? She told you how I married her devoted friend, Jean, and then neglected her and ill-used her and had to be fetched to her deathbed?'

'Yes, she did tell me all that. I didn't particularly want to hear it. I simply wanted to get on with my job.'

'What she didn't tell you was that when I stated my intention of marrying Jean, Eve Wilson, as she then was, became her most deadly enemy. She returned her wedding invitation with a vituperative little note and didn't attend. She behaved with all the concentrated fury of a woman scorned.'

'A woman scorned?' Laura repeated. 'But she's a married woman now.'

'Oh, yes. She very quickly brought her own wedding about. I may be stupidly blind, but apparently my behaviour led her to believe that I favoured her. That is I danced with her sometimes, chatted to her at parties, found her at my side at dinners . . . but I was still shocked and amazed to receive an extremely emotional letter from her, during the period of my short engagement, accusing me of leading her on to expect more, and telling me she would never forget or forgive. In my own happiness I was both sorry for her and surprised that such an apparently attractive girl was driven to abase herself by declaring herself the loser. I would have thought most women would have died rather than admit a passion so secret the other person was not even aware of it. However, my happiness was short-lived. . .'

'You don't have to tell me this,' Laura said uncomfortably.

'I think I do, which is the reason for this date.' Laura flushed in case she should have given the impression that she imagined their date was social. After his experiences

58

with Trevor he obviously believed in putting his intentions clearly into words, and she couldn't blame him. 'When you accepted the job as my ward Sister, after receiving the gipsy's warning, you could only have done so for one of two reasons; either you were dedicated to orthopaedics, or——' he hesitated and she took over.

'Or I calculated that a widower in a state of feud with the other female staff was fair game for attack, eh?'

'I was *not* about to say that,' he chided her.

'Well, if you were, I thought I'd make it easier for you,' she said clearly. 'It's an angle we can't overlook. After all, this is my fifth year in hospitals and I know what goes on. Some doctors are too busy ever to meet any woman other than nurses, and so often they pair off because they talk the same language. I just thought we'd clear that one up. I have no ambitions to become a doctor's wife. Funnily enough, I never had.'

'We'll say that angle's eliminated, then. Now, may I continue?' She nodded coolly and raised her wine-glass. Alcohol really did help to give one assurance, she decided. It had helped her to tell him, in case he had secret suspicions, that she wasn't after him in any way. 'I was about to say that your other reason could have been a sturdy determination to go any way but the one required of you by your colleagues. Some folk can be led but not driven. You may then, having gone your own way, found you had left the frying pan for the fire. I know I'm not an easy person to work for. I drive myself to breaking point and am inclined to forget others are human and, maybe, weaker. When Matron pointed out to me that you are looking paler, thinner and more wan than when you arrived, I realised that you are probably being buffeted from both sides without cease. There is no reason why you should carry on unless you really want to. Sister Trevor's persecution will probably continue, and may become less refined with time. You could get a job elsewhere. Matron would understand and—and so would I.'

'Have you any criticism of the way I run the wards, sir?'

'No. I think you've done wonders. You are marvellous with patients, but have rather less tolerance with their medical advisers.'

'Because I object to rounds in the dinner hour?'

'That, among other things. I told you, I drive myself. My life is nothing but work. I like it that way at the moment, but I know it must make things awkward for one who has been trained to think of the routine as a kind of liturgy which can never be varied. So if there is to be no improvement in the *status quo*, Sister, what would you really like to do? Be frank.'

She took another sip of wine and found she was as articulate and uninhibited as formerly.

'Well, you asked my reasons for taking this particular job, and I'll answer that first. I told Matron I fancied orthopaedics when I knew there was a vacancy, before I knew anything about you or your circumstances. If you had been Richard Burton at his best I wouldn't have been interested just then; though life had to go on my emotions were still tied up with Jim. I had worked and been happiest on orthopaedics. They are always cheerful wards; patients aren't sick in the accepted sense and there's always a lot of chaffing and good humour on both sides. On a chronic sick ward the Sister is often a certain type, a sort of nun-like angel who forms an almost spiritual rapport with her patients; but I didn't see myself like that at all. When I was challenged by Sister Trevor and she automatically assumed I would join her feud by "blacking" your wards, I suppose I did dig my heels in. Nobody chooses my friends and, conversely, nobody tells me who my enemies are, either. So you can conclude that I'm devoted to orthopaedics and I also refuse to be pushed around. I am sorry, of course, to have no friends in the hospital, but we mulish people don't weaken easily. I've stuck it a month and I'll review the situation after a year. Does that answer you, sir?'

He grinned in unwilling admiration.

'She may begin to attack you personally, you know,' he said softly. 'Did you see her expression as we dared dance in answer to her challenge?'

'I did. I feel sorry for her. She must be a very unhappy woman at heart. Maybe she really did love you.'

'This is *love*?' he hooted. 'You have to be joking. I may have been backward, emotionally, for my age, but I loved Jean with a bang the first time she looked on me with any encouragement. We were married within a month. Frankly I hadn't noticed Eve Wilson with my heart at all. She was the sort of girl who traps the eyes, as she intends to, but there is nothing obvious behind the attractive façade. But Jean was one of those nuns you spoke of, quiet and angelic. What I didn't know was that the chap *she* loved had just taken an overseas appointment and left her flat. I came in on the rebound, and we had only lived together for a week before I realised she was having to try awfully hard to tolerate me. When *you* are the lover, all your senses are sharpened to a point where you can tell you are performing a solo. It came out about the other chap, and Jean said she would try. She was fond of me, so if I would give her time . . .?

'I retreated from her turret like a scalded, bewildered cat. There is nothing so damning to a man's ego as to discover his wife wishes he was somebody else. Personally I wanted to call things off, then and there—pride, I suppose—but Jean explained that it would all look rather odd unless we were prepared to leave the country and start afresh. I saw her point. She also sincerely wanted us to be friends, or so she said, though I now think she merely wished to enjoy the social opportunities being married to a rising young specialist afforded her, as a sort of consolation prize for having missed the main chance.

'The truth really came out, however, when from our extremely brief encounter she discovered she was pregnant. I was dismayed, because no matter what arrangement there was between us the door could always remain open barring this one eventuality. She, too, was not only dismayed but extremely vocal about it. I was a lecher and an animal. Only I could have done something like that to her. She valued her figure and her attractions, now she would become fat and ugly and undersirable. I didn't recognise in this virago the woman I had married. She said she would arrange to have an abortion, and I don't know why she never did. She became intimate with Eve Wilson again, and was working part-time at the hospital for a while. I found myself treated as a leper more and more, though I didn't know what Jean was saying about me or what I was supposed to have done. I just worked my energies off flitting from hospital to hospital. I sometimes didn't go home.

'When I did turn up one evening I found another fellow there who turned out to be the escaped lover. After he'd gone I got the full blast of "If only you hadn't married me I would have been free for Miles. Now he can scarcely bear to look at me, all bloated as I am, thanks to you." I told my wife in no uncertain terms that I was no child-snatcher, that she had been free, white and twenty-eight when I proposed to her and that we had been married with all the "trimmings" she craved for in full public view and amid general approbation. I said I was sorry she apparently found me physically repulsive but that it would be a good idea to put the child first rather than allow it to be born into an atmosphere of whining complaint and misery. Could she not see that what was done couldn't now be undone, and that she had helped to do it? I was not very happy, I told her, and she might remember that occasionally. I remember how the fury in her expression destroyed all that nun quality I had loved at first; poor Jean must really have hated me just then. "Perhaps it will make you happier to know that I'm not sure you *are* the father of this child," she screamed at me. "You'll never know for sure. Think about that instead of standing there insulting me!"

'I think I might have strangled her but for the phone ringing at that moment. A boy was haemorrhaging subdurally at Millerdown and they wanted me immediately. I banged out of that damned house and left her, without a word of explanation, determined never to return. The boy—he was sixteen—died on the table and I wondered if I had done all I could, if I wasn't perhaps a degree under par in my job, thanks to my domestic misery. I wandered around for a few hours, went back to look at my patients and was grabbed by somebody who told me I had to go to the Cottage Hospital immediately. My wife, they said, had haemorrhaged severely and was reacting adversely to a transfusion. When I saw her she was limp and white and beautiful again, with all her old serenity somehow restored. The child had been born but she was causing anxiety. She had a common blood group with antibodies which were reacting, and the path people were finding difficulty in cross-matching. She was conscious and wanted to talk. She told me she was sorry I had to suffer, but she hadn't known she was frigid until was too late. "It wasn't you, Jon," she said, "it would have been the same with anybody. I want you to know and forgive me. Please—forgive me." I told her there was nothing to forgive and to buck up and get better. I was shoved out, then, while they tried another transfusion, but when they called me back inside she was obviously dying, and in ten minutes it was all over.

'They wanted me to get all excited about the baby, but I couldn't. I may have been dotty, but I had just lost the only woman I had ever wanted to look at twice, and it's odd how you forget the bad bits so quickly. Talking about the baby brought a bad bit back, however. If it was a full term baby, then it wasn't mine, and rather than know the worst I walked out leaving him to the midwives.

'That's about all there is to tell. I've told you all because Jean may have confided more than I know to her cronies, and I've been like a bad smell to the Sisters' Common Room at the Cottage ever since. If you've heard other versions of my story, well, it's only right you should hear mine, and then you'll know the sort of chap you're tagging along with. I closed that unhappy house down and took the flat I'm in now. I placed Simon with a couple I know. He's a fine little chap; has his first birthday next week. I must look that up and clear some time.'

Laura was dying to know if he knew the baby to be his own son, but as he spoke like any proud father, she was afraid to stir things up again.

'Thanks for telling me, sir,' she said at length. 'You didn't have to, because it wouldn't have made any difference to me, but the other version I heard was rather weighted against you. However, I happen to believe in being allowed to work where I'm needed, even if Lucifer himself happens to be in charge.' They both smiled at that analogy.

'Actually I left my toasting fork in the Jag,' he said.

'I'm sorry,' she added awkwardly, 'that you were so unhappy.'

'So were you.'

'Yes. But that was different. . . .'

'I agree. Better, they say, to have loved and lost than never to have loved at all, but I wonder. . . Anyhow, it was a great inoculation. I shall never catch it again.'

'For different reasons, neither will I. Mine was too perfect to much, while yours was disillusionment after disillusionment.'

'Dr Warwick?' a waiter was bowing.

'Yes?'

'I have someone on the phone for you, Doctor, in the manager's office. This way, please.'

Laura watched him go wondering what it must be like for a normal, healthy man to find the woman he has married visibly shrinking away from contact with him.

'How awful!' she pondered. 'How terrible for him! I must try to understand how it is with him that he's always popping up at annoying times. I mustn't add to his troubles. He's just working out all his frustrations, I suppose. What a pity if he never meets the right woman, who would understand and repair his faith in our sex.'

It may have been that Laura's emotions had been sharpened either by the wine or by the preceding unhappy confidences of her companion, but for a few moments she drifted into a daydream where she saw quite clearly a picture which had been eluding her for some time, that of Jim's happy, laughing countenance as it had been when he had looked round for her, maybe after the triumph of a rugby game his team had won. At such times his glance had sought her dispassionately, content to know that she was there and his mind already on the shower he was about to enjoy and the glass of beer which always tasted so good before the 'boys' dispersed to take up their men's affairs once again. As Laura gobbled up this unexpected vision she also knew it was goodbye to the past. Wherever one went to, Jim had gone, and knowing him and his thirst for life and experience she wouldn't expect him to hang about waiting for her. He faded as she stared, unwinkingly, and a sterner countenance took his place, piercing blue eyes questioned the blankness of her gaze.

'Are you all right, Sister?'

She blinked a few times. 'Yes, I'm all right. I was just thinking. Are you needed? Is there an emergency?'

'Hardly that. It's the kid, Simon. He's playing up Bob and Katie, seems feverish. Katie thinks it might be a tooth and the local doctor's out delivering a baby, so she wonders if I would just call in and take a look at him. Would you mind terribly if we popped over to Oldport before I deliver you back at the hospital?'

'Not at all. That's the pretty little village with the old land-locked harbour, isn't it? I walked there once, on my day off.'

'Walked?' he echoed. 'It must be seven miles.'

'I walked back again, too. I like walking.'

'So do I. But after ward duty that makes you a positive heroine.' She had thrilled to the unexpected touch of his hand on her shoulder before she realised they were pas-

65

sing Eve Trevor's party and this must be for the benefit of their common persecutor. He removed it as they reached neutral territory and she told herself it was only the surprise which was accountable for the response of her nerves. She was not, repeat *was not* looking for anyone to take Jim's place in her heart or life.

The road to Oldport village was narrow, winding and unlit, and so Jon drove carefully and Laura did not attempt to distract him with conversation.

Oldport smelled of seaweed and fishing tackle and tar, though the old industries were no longer viable hereabouts. It was an old stone-built village where retired people from the nearest town often chose to live. It was not beautiful, and was often lashed by gales, but it had the reputation of being healthy, especially for bronchitics and asthmatics.

'Bob Barnes is a journalist and was my best man,' Jon Warwick explained. 'Kate's an American. They have no children of their own after eight years of marriage. That's the way the cookie crumbles, as Kate would say.'

When they reached the converted harbour-master's house which was the Barnes' home, Laura was introduced to the very pleasant couple as 'Sister Bradfield'.

'Oooh!' exclaimed Kate meaningfullyy.

'Nothing like that, as she will assure you,' Jon said quickly, and everybody laughed, including Laura.

The baby was sitting on a rug in front of the guarded fire banging a wooden spoon on a cake tin. He looked full of beans and was a sturdy little fair boy. Laura had hoped to tell at a glance that he was Jon's son, but she couldn't. He had whitish-silver sort of hair which many babies grow after losing the tufts they are born with. He didn't look like being a dark boy, ever, and though his eyes were blue they were more of a violet shade. Jon's eyes were so sky-blue they were a commanding feature. The boy must take after his mother, or—she suppressed the rest of her thoughts. They didn't help anyone.

Simon obviously adored his father, though probably

more in the light of an indulgent stranger who occasionally came to see him and played with him. When he hit his chubby fingers with the spoon, by mistake, his open mouth squared towards Kate, who was immediately sympathetic, and then he gave his fingers to Bob to kiss better, too.

'How can he bear,' thought Laura, with a pang, 'to have his child with other people!'

She couldn't immediately see how he could do otherwise; she didn't know if there were any grandparents or not, and to leave Simon with a housekeeper all day long would deny him the family atmosphere in which a young child thrived.

'There doesn't seem to be a thing wrong with this joker,' Jon said at length, having made his son laugh again. 'He just doesn't seem to be tired.'

'No, well—' Kate said defensively '—he slept all afternoon from two o'clock until six. He had a rather disturbed night with his last tooth, but it's through now, so I let him sleep.'

'Then you can't expect the kid to——'Jon remonstrated, and then saw that Kate was biting her lip rather nervously.

'You haven't seen him in such ages,' she said, 'and I thought it was time. You know how you are, Jon. It's got to be an emergency before even a friend can get hold of you nowadays. We wanted to see you. Bob has something to tell you.'

'Oh?' questioned Jon.

'Come on into the study,' invited the other, and the two men disappeared.

'I'll bring us some coffee,' Kate told Laura, 'then Simon simply *must* go to bed. I need my sleep, if he doesn't!'

They chatted, as they sipped the coffee, about children in general and Simon in particular.

'He's at such a cute age,' Kate said adoringly. 'He tries to say Mommy, I know he does. Bob says it's just a noise, but I can tell. Do you think he should be talking by now, Sister?'

'They vary so much,' Laura said. 'He's a bit young to say much more than jumbles at the moment, but there's no doubt he has a special sound just for you. This coming year he'll develop in every way.'

'Yes. It worries me, sometimes, how much joy Jon is missing.'

When the men emerged from the study, Simon was in his cot and fast asleep. Jon went in to see him and came out frowning thoughtfully.

'Well, I'll make the party if I possibly can,' he told his friends. 'I promise you that. Remind me, Sister, my son has a first birthday party next Wednesday, would you? I'll let you know about the other matter,' he tossed over his shoulder, and after exchanging goodnights the visitors left the house.

It was raining by now, off the sea, cold, stinging lances with a threat of winter about them.

'Have you home by half past eleven,' Jon promised. 'I hope that's all right?'

'Oh, yes. My pass extends until twelve.'

'Oh, then would you care for a final drink at my place? The pubs will all be shut by now.'

'Oh no, thank you,' said Laura, a little embarrassed. 'One has to allow for all eventualities when one has a date with a man like you. The only time I ever before went out with a doctor our evening didn't start till after ten. He was an obstetrical registrar and that happened to be a busy evening for him.'

'I once thought I might be an obstetrician. Then I became fascinated by E.N.T. work. I was attached to a Hungarian specialist who didn't think much of my chances, however. 'Ach, boy,' he said too me, 'the human belly is big. You can drop retractors right into it and take zem out again. But the human ear is small and delicate as a Sviss vatch. You take your big hands avay and go and find a belly surgeon!' So I did the next best thing and

68

joined an orthopaedic team.'

Laura laughed and stepped out of the car outside the nurses' home.

'Thank you for a very pleasant evening, sir,' she said sincerely. 'I may still resist you on occasions, but at least I'll understand why you mess up my routine. Simon's a lovely child. It was nice seeing him.'

'Yes, it was,' he said rather flatly. 'Goodnight, Sister,' and he drove away without more ado.

Next morning she had a visitor. It was Tony's mother and there was a harsh light in the woman's eyes.

'Calling yourself a nurse!' she said harshly. 'You should be ashamed!'

'What have I done, Mrs Devon? Please be calm. Don't shout.'

'Don't shout, you say! I feel like shouting what I have to say from the housetops. Look at that! Just look at that!' she tossed a sheet of paper down on the desk. 'And they put you in charge of my poor helpless boy!'

Laura dumbly read the evil printed capitals on the notepaper in front of her.

DID YOU KNOW THAT SISTER BRADFIELD WAS DISMISSED FROM HER LAST HOSPITAL FOR CAUSING THE DEATH OF A PATIENT? SHE WAS SUPPOSED TO LOOK AFTER YOUR SON *SPECIALLY*. WHY DON'T YOU CONSIDER SUEING HER OR THE HOSPITAL? A SYMPATH-ETIC FRIEND.

Laura felt physically sick for a moment.

'Well?' asked the woman. 'Do you deny what it says? Do you?'

'An anonymous letter?' Laura asked. 'Why doesn't your sympathetic friend sign her name?'

'How do you know it's a woman, eh?'

'*I* could put a name to it and be ninety-nine per cent certain I was right. I'm disgusted. You have enough trouble and sorrow without anybody adding to it.'

'But what about what it says, eh? Do you deny it?'

'Every word,' Laura said. She took the newspaper cutting out of her locker. 'That's what happened, if you want to know, and I wasn't dismissed. I resigned from my last hospital. I made one mistake, yes, I admit. I had just been told my fiancé was dead at twenty-four. I've certainly paid for what I did, but whoever wrote that letter to you wasn't being any friend of yours, but trying to do me further harm. I can tell you sincerely, Mrs Devon, that all was done for Tony that could humanly be done. Please believe that. Not for one moment did I see him unhappy; everybody liked and admired his spirit. Any acrimony or vindictiveness, now, can only mar the remembrance we have of a very brave boy.'

'Yes, I suppose so.' The woman suddenly sagged. 'Nothing'll bring Tony back, anyway. I'm sorry, Sister. I'd like to tell whoever wrote this what I think of them. Would you tell me who you suspect?'

'Well, I think you're a bit emotional at the moment, Mrs Devon, and it is only a suspicion, in any case. May I keep the note, please? If any more of these appear in circulation I would rather act myself. Now let me make you a cup of tea, and——'

'No, thanks, Sister. I've taken up enough of your time already. I have to get on with living, somehow. But after what you went through you'll know all about that,' she ventured shyly.

'Yes, I do. And the worst gets over and time does heal. Goodbye, then, Mrs Devon.'

'Goodbye, Sister. I'm that sorry I burst in on you like I did.'

'We were both meant to be upset. In that way your unknown correspondent can be satisfied. I think it's best, however, to forget it if we can.'

When the woman had left, however, Laura found herself actually trembling. She had never been hated before, to her knowledge, and this methodical seeking out of all her vulnerable places was frightening. Did Eve Trevor so badly wish to see her hounded out of the cottage hospital, even though it took a lawsuit to do it? As Jon Warwick had warned her, the attacks were now becoming more personal and subtle. How could one fight the evil openly that attacked in secret and under cover of anonymity?

She folded the horrid letter up in the newspaper cutting and put both items away together. At this rate no patient in her care could die of natural causes without fear of their relatives being informed of the one slip marring her otherwise immaculate career. She was not the type whose nature is to hit back when attacked and join battle. She merely wished to be left in peace and do her job. But she was terribly shaken. After Amanda's attack, and now Mrs Devon's, she wondered if she might be driven to resigning for the hospital's sake. No hospital can afford the trouble caused by unnecessary enquiries or lawsuits, and the letter in her possession was inciting for incitement's sake. It was vicious and horrid and she must try to forget it. The only way to do that was to fill one's head with patients and their needs. She had a fellow-feeling with Jon Warwick as she realised he, too, had been driven by disagreeable circumstances into doing likewise.

Doing her mail round, Laura realized how fond she had become of these patients. Even Jim Potts now greeted her appearance cheerfully. For the first time she saw him looking normal, his countenance not drawn by constant, unaccountable, often severe pain. His right leg, in a long plaster, was dangling from a cradle in a bandage sling.

'My word, Sister,' he greeted her, 'I slept all night like a baby. It's wonderful.'

'So the plaster helps, eh?'

'I'll say. Why didn't I have a plaster before? It was hell for weeks. When I remember——' and he frowned again.

'You had a rather nasty ulcer, Jim, and we had to get that better first. The plaster's fine for the knee, but if you start to ulcerate anywhere you must let me know immediately. O.K.?'

'But then what, Sister? All that pain again?'

'No, no, I hope not. We would have to cut a window in the plaster to dress the ulcer. But maybe you're on the way up now, eh? The fitter you get the less chance there is of these things happening. So eat and exercise and keep your spirits up.'

In the women's ward Mrs Kershaw was getting ready to be transferred to Millerdown for an operation on her deformed feet.

'My goodness, Sister, I'm that excited!'

'Now don't you get too excited, my dear. You're not going to the circus.'

'No, better'n that. When I see you again it'll all be over. Think of that!'

'I am, and I still want you to calm down a bit. In case I don't get the chance to have a word with you before they come for you, all my love and best wishes.'

'Oh, Sister!' Mrs Kershaw's washed-out eyes welled with tears. 'It was you made it all possible. It was you.'

'Now, none of that! I believe the porters are coming for you now. They'll think you don't want to go if they see those tears. Now I'm relying on you to keep your own end up and Mr Warwick will see to the rest. I'll be asking about you.'

Everybody liked Mrs Kershaw and there were sentimental goodbyes as she was wheeled out of the ward on her great adventure.

'Goodbye!' called Amanda, more shrilly than all. 'I'll remember what you told me! Good luck!'

Mr Warwick was actually on time for the round and it passed without untoward incident. As she made his coffee in the office afterwards, he told her he was sending her another spinal case in the male ward.

'Oh, no!' she groaned. 'Not another young boy, I hope?'

'Mid-twenties. Motor-cycle maniac. Deep coma—too deep. His wife sits with him by the hour, though what miracle she expects I can't imagine. Well, Sister,' he said kindly, 'I can't keep him at Millerdown indefinitely, now can I?'

'No, of course not. It's just that we're still upset about Tony, I suppose. When will he be coming?'

'This afternoon. The bed he's on will stay here and send yours back with the ambulance. Well, I think that's all.'

'You asked me to remind you, sir, about your son's birthday.' His eyes grew round and disbelieving. 'It's today,' she told him. 'Had you forgotten?'

'Oh, lord!'

'I hope you're free this evening?'

'Yes. Yes, I think I am. Up to now I am. But I haven't bought him anything.'

'You can be too busy for your own good,' she chided him. 'I have two hours off this afternoon. Can I help?'

'I say, would you?'

'I'd better have the shop deliver it direct. Now will you remember you have a date this evening? You did promise.'

'Well, maybe you could come along to remind me——?' his gaze wavered on her unwinking brown orbs.

'They'd think it odd, wouldn't they? Your ward Sister, twice? In any case I'm on late duty and I think by then I'll have a headache.'

He apparently didn't notice the cynical observation, for he was looking at a sheet of paper in his hand. 'Now I understand why Sister Trevor sent me a Valentine, today,' he said wryly. 'This was in my pigeon-hole. She must have every date, every anniversary carefully filed away to suitably remind me of my supposed defection from her grace.' He handed the sheet to Laura, who was struck by the perfume accompanying it, firstly, and then by the texture of the paper itself.

'On this day of shame' (was written) 'I hope your head hangs low. How all women should despise you!'

'Are you sure Sister Trevor wrote this?' asked Laura.

'Yes. She has written me previously. I told you.'

'Then—' Laura fished out the anonymous letter, printed on identical perfumed paper '—she has started writing to others. Tony's mother presented me with this.'

Jon looked serious as he read.

'The vixen!' he exclaimed. 'I think we're going to have to present this correspondence to Matron, the hospital committee. It's gone beyond bounds with this.'

'No. No, don't do that,' Laura said quickly. 'If she lost her job she would hate us none the less and I believe she's a good theatre Sister. Would you—let me handle it, please, sir?'

'Well——'

'*Please!*' she urged.

'O.K. If there's any more of it, though, we've got to kick her where it really hurts. I won't have this anonymous scandalmongering from anybody.'

Sometimes Laura had dinner in her room, with a book for company, but the next day she took her place at the Sister's table and started with apparently good appetite on the steak and kidney pie.

Trevor had been telling the others about a wedding she had attended, but this subject was dropped and she started her usual baiting.

'Talking of weddings makes you think of deaths, doesn't it? It's a year since poor Jean died, neglected by that devil of a husband of hers.'

'He did come when he knew,' expostulated Martyn. 'He was quite upset.'

'Oh, poor thing!' said Trevor. 'She was dying and he was upset. Maybe he had a date she was keeping him from.'

'There's no need to talk like that to me,' Sister Martyn said coldly. 'I'm only stating the facts. I was very fond of Sister Yorke.'

'We all were. She was one of us. If you ask me, it's a sin he's still walking around this hospital after what he did.'

'Perhaps he's doing a good job of work,' Laura said to

74

no one in particular. 'He's getting on with the present instead of dwelling in the past, which does nobody any good.'

'Was that mice?' asked Trevor, after a pregnant silence, but for once nobody tittered.

'No, it was one of your colleagues who dares to have a mind of her own and form her own judgements about people. There's a great deal of small-mindedness goes on at this table, which I find truly amazing when I realize the company is supposed to be adult, and hospital Sisters into the bargain.'

'Well——!' Sister Martyn said offendedly.

'Now, don't answer her,' warned Trevor. 'That's what she's after, to break Coventry.'

'I couldn't care less about being in Coventry. It no longer punishes me and only belittles you. I have no desire to be your friend and intimate, Sister Trevor. You have proved yourself to be self-opinionated, spiteful, underhand and mean.'

'Now she insults me,' said Trevor icily, 'She thinks I'll talk to her, if only to quarrel.'

'Still,' said Mahmoud, 'it is terrible to have someone think such things about you. I would want to know, "Why do you say such things? What am I doing to deserve this?" '

'She knows,' Laura pressed on, still not looking at anybody. 'I think it's pitiful when a person of supposed intelligence sends miserable anonymous letters around.'

Trevor went first pale and her green eyes narrowed, then she decided to bluster.

'I never sent an anonymous letter in my life,' she said virtuously. 'I don't know what she's talking about.'

'This is what I'm talking about,' Laura said, and handed a sheet of paper to Sister Martyn, who was nearest. She read the missive and then said, looking round the table,

'You must have written this, Eve, because it's about Jean dying. Only you remembered the exact date and it's

75

written on notepaper I gave you last Christmas.'

Eve snatched the note and said fiercely, 'Of course I wrote that. I wrote it to *him* to let him know we hadn't forgotten. I don't call that anonymous. *He* knows darned well who wrote it.'

'And this?' Laura passed the other note to Martyn, who read it, passed it on to Mahmoud, Jepson, Saunders and finally to Trevor herself.

'I didn't send *this*,' she said sharply, 'though I agree with every word it says.'

'Of course you sent it,' Martyn said grimly. 'It's on the same notepaper and I recognise your printing. You did some invitations in that script once. If you ask me it's all getting a bit out of hand.'

'All right,' Trevor suddenly shrilled, 'so I thought that poor woman wanted putting wise. Any harm in that?'

'If I'd had anything to say I'd have said it in person,' Martyn said stoutly. 'It all seems sneaky and horrid done that way, as though even you are ashamed of what you're doing.'

'So I'm all wrong, now, am I? Go on over to her, then, and send me to Coventry. I'm a rotter. Does that satisfy you? Damn you all!' and Trevor leapt up from the table and marched out of the room.

'And she hasn't had her coffee yet,' said Sister Mahmoud, shaking her pretty head.

'I don't want to come between old friends,' Laura said clearly, 'so I'll go now, and maybe you can persuade her to come back.'

'No, don't go,' said Martyn quickly and it was the first time she had addressed Laura personally in weeks. 'There's no need for you to run away. It's your dining-table as much as ours.'

'Please, have we stopped going to Coventry?' asked Mahmoud, pleasantly.

'I suppose all that *was* a bit childish,' admitted Martyn.

'I never held with it from the start,' said Sister Saunders, adjusting her hearing-aid. 'A lot of newfangled nonsense is what I call it.'

'Well, my mama always says,' Jamaican Jepson volunteered, 'that nobody's all lily-white and so there must be give and take.'

'How could you be lily-white, isn't it?' chuckled Mahmoud, and soon all were laughing, including Laura and Jepson loudest of all. It felt good to be one of a crowd again, even though one was on the outer edge of it.

'Perhaps Sister Trevor will come back if I go.' Laura said at length. 'I'm sorry if I've caused trouble, but it seemed the only way to stop the menace of those letters. Mr Warwick wanted to put them before the hospital committee, but I think they're best kept in the family, don't you?'

She picked up both letters from the table and tore them into scraps.

'We'll see there are no more letters,' promised Martyn.

'Thank you,' and giving a brief nod to the table at large, Laura made her departure without more ado.

CHAPTER FOUR

LAURA decided to go home for her first long weekend off duty. Her home was in Oxfordshire, in a pleasant village within commuting distance of London. She had imagined she would enjoy the break more than she actually did, however. Home had seemed so wonderful to anticipate when she was a young student nurse, and she had been terribly sick for it for almost a year. Now, however, not only the house but Cobwick itself seemed much smaller, in spite of the housing estates which were encroaching over farmland she remembered. She had attended her first dance with a member of the Young Farmers' Club, and now she couldn't remember what Gerry Burgess had looked like, only the absurdity of a button flying off his well-filled dinner-jacket remained with her to this day. Of course her mother wanted to fatten her up, and scarcely left the kitchen during the whole of her daughter's stay.

'You can take back to hospital what you can't eat here,' Mrs Bradfield asserted, when Laura remarked on the trays of queen cakes set out on racks to cool.

It was pleasant taking Lassie, the black labrador bitch, for walks. Lassie loved the long tramps her young mistress was fond of, too. She had the true labrador's deep chest and a capacity for jogging along by the hour, occasionally flashing off after imaginary rabbits and flushing innocent blackbirds from coverts mistakenly for pheasant.

Coming home for Sunday lunch, after such a tramp, Laura was surprised to see young Dr Wales propping up the chimney-piece smoking a pipe. Derek was the local doctor's son, and had at one time resisted working in the family practice. She had imagined Derek to be in the Antipodes somewhere.

'Hello, Derek!' she greeted. 'It isn't Daddy's asthma, is it? He was all right when I went out.'

'I—er——'

'I invited Derek to lunch before I knew you were coming home,' Mrs Bradfield said. 'I don't think he's eaten in this house since he used to hang about the gate on baking days,' and she smiled at Derek indulgently while avoiding her daughter's eye, so that Laura knew Derek had been invited deliberately. Her mother had known for a month that she would be home on her long weekend.

Even after the meal, when Mrs Bradfield insisted on doing the washing up herself, and shooing her husband off for his nap, Laura felt embarrassed at the too-obvious tactics.

'Parents!' she said with a grimace. 'They try eternally, don't they? I'm sorry, Derek, if Mother really bulldozed you into this lunch party.'

'Oh, gracious, Laura, it's been nice seeing you again. I heard when I was down under about your Jim. I'm awfully sorry. I had an unhappy ending to my love-affair, too. She married another.'

'*C'est la vie, et c'est l'amour,*' Laura shrugged. 'Are you working with your father now?'

'Only till I get fixed up. Cobwick stifles me nowadays.'

'Me, too. When I left my last hospital Mother wanted me to try to get work on the district, living at home. I know I was upset at the time, but I simply couldn't tolerate the idea. I would have smothered.'

'If you'll take it in the spirit I intend it, Laura, you're vastly improved, you know.'

'Improved?' Laura asked blankly.

'You're prettier. Much prettier than I remember you.'

'You mean those long plaits you described, unflatteringly, as cows' tails?' she dimpled.

'I didn't, did I?'

'Yes, you did. I hated you more than any other boy I knew, Derek Wales.'

'That's a blow. I was terribly in love with you when I was sixteen. You'd just been bobbed and your hair used to shine in the sunlight, and surely the sun always shone those days? Mind you, there wasn't a lot of female competition in Cobwick at the time. Do you remember Myrtle Fayne with her fat legs and adolescent spots?'

'Poor Myrtle! She bought everything for her spots ever produced in a pharmacy. The last I heard of Myrtle she was happily married and had a bouncing boy, so the spots must have gone eventually.'

'And we're both of us on the shelf, or should I speak only for myself?'

'No, I'm there, too, but quite willingly. I'm sure there'll be someone else for you eventually, Derek. Your pride's a bit hurt at the moment.'

'Not to mention my self-confidence. How can one be sure it won't happen the same way again?'

'One can't, obviously, but one can't hide away like a hermit, either.'

'There's a girl I met only last week and—you know, eyes across a crowded room, and all that? I was so sick with nervousness, however, that I didn't follow it up. I could kick myself.'

'Nobody will know about the other business unless you advertise it yourself, you know. The fact that you can feel attracted again shows that you've got over it. Forget it.'

'What sort of quality in a man would you look for, apart from natural attraction, that is?'

'I would want him to be honest with me more than anything. When a man is devious about anything you immediately suspect him in every way.'

'Aunt Laura's advice to the lovelorn! Thank you. I hope you're not on that shelf too long yourself, either. It would be a waste. Well, much as I've enjoyed this reunion, my dear, I must push off now. I told Dad I'd give a couple of injections in the village. So long, Laura, and all the best.'

He stooped to kiss her as a brother might, just as Mrs Bradfield rejoined them, looking immediately coy.

'He's grown into such a nice young man, has Derek,'

she sighed happily as he went down the path to his car. 'Aren't you glad I asked him, dear?'

'Very glad, you sly puss, but it wasn't love at second sight despite your contriving. Now I must get my things together and start back. Perhaps Dad will drive me to the station?'

'I'm sure he will. Are you really over that business, Laura? Tell me truly.'

'Of course I am, Mother. Don't fret about me.'

'And you like your new job?'

'Love it.'

'Are there any nice young doctors?'

'A few, but they're nearly all married.'

'Oh. Mrs Willis, my daily, read my teacup the other morning. You know how we used to laugh at her predictions together? Well, she said she could see a wedding in the family of someone very close to me, and that it would be sudden and unexpected and cause a deal of pother. Her very words.'

'Why should it be me?' Laura smiled teasingly.

'Because there's nobody else near to me who isn't married already. You don't suppose your Uncle Fred would take such a step at his age, do you?'

'Why not? That would be enough to cause all the pother you speak of. In any case, we always laughed at Mrs Willis and her tea-leaves before, so why not this time?'

'Maybe, I hope for you, Laura. Hope that some nice young man will touch your heart and lead you into all the happiness I've known with your father.'

'Well, thanks, Mum. I can't see it happening just yet, but you never know. Now how about packing up those spare queen cakes for me? I'm going to give them out with teas tomorrow to my long-term patients who have forgotten what home-baked goodies taste like.'

Jon Warwick was scowling and obviously in a bad mood. His 'Good morning, Sister. So you got back all right?'

was said in such a way as not to merit a reply, so she kept silent as she tagged along after his flying white coat, signalling to a nurse to fetch the trolley on which were laid the patients' notes in neat files.

'I didn't know you were going off like that,' he said between wards. 'If I was told it didn't register.'

'Well, *you* weren't in on Friday, sir,' she reminded him, 'but it was my sixth weekend and I was due for a break. I left everything in order, didn't I?' she asked.

'I suppose so.' They had reached the spinal bed with Roger still lying, a mangled vegetable of a man, unconscious upon it. Nurse O'Connell had whisked the young wife, Marjorie, away for the duration of the round. Jon lifted an eyelid, used his stethoscope, and shook his head. 'Do you know they can live for years like that?' he observed, though Laura knew well enough. 'If it's a pretty girl the papers call her "Sleeping Beauty", or some such thing. It is true, though, that the ageing process seems to be slowed down. Now look at Roger. He's quite good-looking, isn't he? Greek god-like. Waxen and as good as dead. I can't make that wife of his see it. She wants me to tell her he'll rise one day, like Lazarus, and he won't. She ought to go out and find another man——'

'Sir!' Laura objected sternly.

'Oh, I'm sorry if that sounded immoral. But she's normal and healthy and she can't remain tied to that poor wreck and keep her reason.'

'Maybe she has enough happy memories on which to survive. Maybe it's the sort of love normal people fail to comprehend.'

'Maybe, and amen. You *have* come back in a mood, haven't you?'

'I've come back in a mood?' Laura nearly squeaked. It was the first time she was near to quarrelling with Jon Warwick since their new-found understanding. She controlled herself with difficulty and the round proceeded without further untoward event. She would have liked to sulk and not make his coffee, but he sat down so obviously to wait that she plugged the kettle in and ladled instant coffee into two cups.

'I tried to phone you on Saturday,' he said suddenly. 'I wanted to talk to somebody and I thought you might have been interested.'

'Oh?' she poured boiling water on to the coffee and when it foamed a little added milk and sugar. 'Did you find somebody else, then?'

'No. I didn't bother.'

'Then do you want to tell me now?'

'No. There isn't time, and I don't like discussing private business when I'm paid to be on duty.'

'Well—' she gave a gesture of helplessness '—do you want to tell me some other time, or not?'

He rose, as she thought, maddeningly.

'Bad moods are catching,' he remarked as she began to smoulder again. 'We'll change the subject. There's a very select dinner takes place on Founder's Day, which is next Friday evening. Medical staff and senior nursing staff only. I didn't attend last year because of my domestic troubles. Matron has said she expects me this year. One is supposed to take one's ward Sister. I suppose that's O.K. by you?'

'I was reading on the notice board that formal attire is requested. I suppose I'll see you there, in that case, sir.'

'I was trying,' he actually looked somewhat embarrassed, 'to assure you that you would at least have somebody to talk to.'

'Oh. Oh!' she suddenly saw the light. 'Actually the worst of that is over, sir. Most of my colleagues now do talk to me.'

'That's good. That's very good. Right. I'll push along, then, Sister.'

She wondered, when he had gone, why he should have tried to contact her on Saturday night. She had been at home, watching television, trying not to think she was bored. What could he have wanted to talk to her about? The more she thought about it the more she wished she had been there. If his intention had been to rouse her curiosity then he had succeeded.

On Friday morning young Amanda Wade was due for discharge. She could now walk competently on crutches, and though she would attend as an outpatient for months, maybe, even, for years, there was no point in hospitalising the girl further. The staff nurse was having her day off, and so Laura was short-handed and was packing the girl's things for her, while her mother helped her to dress behind screens.

'Oh, Mum!' Laura heard the familiar complaining voice. 'You're hurting me. Stop it! I can manage myself.'

Mrs Wade came tight-lipped from behind the screen.

'I've always done everything for that girl,' she told Laura, 'now she's suddenly independent. It makes me feel unnecessary.'

'I should encourage her to be independent,' Laura advised. 'When she can literally stand unaided on her own two feet again, she'll need the mental equipment to go with it.'

Amanda came out dressed in a frock she had obviously outgrown. 'We'll have to go shopping, Mum,' she said wryly. 'Just look at me!'

'You can have what you like, love. In reason,' added Mrs Wade, noting Sister's frown. 'I'll just see if your dad's downstairs with the car.'

'Well, Mandy,' Laura said brightly, 'looking forward to getting home again?'

'Yes and no, Sister. In a way I've liked it here, especially lately when things started to happen so fast.'

'You made them happen, Mandy. You started to fight back.'

'Yes, I—I suppose I did. You made me mad on purpose, didn't you, Sister? You knew what it would do to me.'

'It was a chance we had to take. It came off in your case.'

'But I was so awful to you. I didn't realise. I—I'm sorry if I said anything to upset you, Sister. Mrs Kershaw made me see I was wrong.'

'That's all right, Mandy. We'll forgive and forget.'

'I'll never forget. Can I come and see you sometimes?'

'Why not? But only when there's a marked improvement in your condition so that I can tell you're remembering other things I said, too, like never giving in until you're as near a hundred per cent as possible.'

'I'll make it a hundred and one per cent, Sister. Just for you.' They both laughed. 'Ah, there's my daddy. I must go.'

Laura stooped swiftly and kissed the girl.

'Come on! I'll take you all down in the lift.'

Having seen the Wades off the premises, Laura returned to the ward thinking about the absent Mrs Kershaw, who was not recovering as well after operations on her feet as had been hoped. For one thing she was a slow healer and did not respond to modern wonder drugs like most people. She would probably be coming back to the Cottage Hospital any day.

Though it was snug in the wards it was a bitterly cold day out of doors, with a high wind and lashing, squally showers. At dinner the other senior staff had been discussing the Founder's Day celebration that evening.

'It's a feed, anyway,' Sister Martyn said philosophically, 'and providing that's good one simply has to endure the wretched speeches. What are you wearing, Trevor?'

'Green, to match my eyes.' Jepson laughed. 'I want to look slinky for old Philber.'

Mr Philber was the senior abdominal surgeon in the group and most of his operations were done at the Cottage.

'What are you wearing tonight, Sister Bradfield?' asked Mahmoud politely.

'I haven't really thought about it,' Laura answered. 'I have a black dress, but I had really intended to go shopping. Now it's too late.'

'Still, natural blondes always look well in black,' Mahmoud added, and there was a somewhat embarrassed pause, for it was common knowledge that Sister Trevor's cream-coloured locks were not natural and she was easily huffed.

Of all the Sisters, Trevor had not yet voluntarily spoken to Laura. If there was something of an official nature to be discussed, then she said only what was necessary, and if Laura tried to add anything personal, such as thanks or even a reference to the weather, it was more than likely to be ignored, so there was no use in trying to force the pace.

Laura was relieved by Sister Grantham, a part-timer who occasionally helped out when there was load-shedding to be done. She went to prepare for the function ahead, really feeling bored by the whole prospect. She would rather have settled down with the Graham Greene novel she had been fortunate in finding in the hospital library, but Matron had already intimated that she expected a full attendance by invited staff.

Laura donned her black evening dress, glad of the silver lamé bolero which complemented it so well on cold evenings. Her hair, newly washed, was too soft to hold in the usual pleat, so she gathered it up into a chignon and thought, rather glumly, what a waste it all was for an esoteric gathering such as a hospital's senior staff, where even the jokes would have a medical flavour and probably be old chestnuts in any case. A tap on her door made her heart lift, slightly. It would be like old times if Mahmoud or Martyn dropped in to ask her to hook them up, or help them with their hair. More than anything else, such a gesture would make her feel finally accepted as one of them. But it was Home Sister, elderly and thin, who stood there in a grey velvet dress which did nothing for her parchment complexion.

'I have Mr Warwick downstairs for you, Sister. Are you ready?'

'Surely I'm not late?' asked Laura, who hadn't expected literally to be escorted to the dinner. A bus was supposed to be collecting them at eight and she made it seven-fifteen.

'Mr Warwick said he'd be glad if you could join him immediately, Sister. What shall I tell him? You *do* look nice, I may add. So young.'

'Thank you, Sister. You look very nice, too. I only have to collect my coat and bag, so I'll be down in a minute.'

Feeling uncertain, Laura descended the stairs, feeling the blue eyes upon her rather than seeing them.

'I didn't know you——' she ventured rather lamely.

His arm under her elbow hustled her outside. 'I couldn't have planned to get through so early myself, but I took a chance on you being ready. After all, you haven't much to do to yourself. Not like some women.'

'Whatever do you mean by that, Mr Warwick?' she asked as he opened the door of the Jag and handed her inside.

He appeared in the driving seat and said, 'I meant nothing unflattering. I don't believe in being devious. You're a good-looking woman and you don't plaster yourself up with a lot of unnecessary goo. Your hair's nice,' he added. 'Simple, yet nice. That's what I meant. You don't have to go to a great deal of trouble to achieve an effect.'

She smiled in the darkness. 'Mr Warwick, I don't have to be coy with you, but I must be honest. For a solid hour I've tried my hair this way and that to achieve the effect of simplicity and naturalness. I spend as much time on my appearance as most women. I even use goo, though as it doesn't suit my type I wash most of it off again before zero hour. That probably makes me a coward.'

'I wonder——' he commented.

'By the way,' she said, 'aren't we going to be very early at this dinner?'

'I thought we'd have an aperitif first. I want to make a suggestion to you.'

'That sounds ominous, sir.'

'It is. How's your digestion, Sister? I don't want to upset it.'

'Now what sort of suggestion *could* upset my digestion? I'm hungry—in fact ravenous—and my gastric juices are working normally. You're not going to upset the ward routine more than usually, are you?'

'That may be indirectly involved. Anyway, here's my favourite little pub and we may get near the fire at this time.'

It was cosy in the Anchor Inn bar-parlour, with rain lashing against the leaded windows and hissing in the log fire. Not another soul was present as Jon ordered a dry Martini and a medium sherry.

'Now,' he said, as the drinks arrived, 'why not to us?' he raised his glass. 'The Old Founder, whoever he was, and rest his soul, will get his share later. To the new team,' he suggested, and to that they drank.

'You may think I'm out of my mind,' he proceeded, 'but I have given a great deal of thought to what I'm about to propose. In case you think I have numerous alternatives, I would explain that I have no parents or near relatives. An uncle brought me up and he is now living in retirement in the Caribbean. He was a bachelor G.P. and I've known no close relationships with women, apart from my wife, and you know that was neither long nor—very close. I don't think I have acquired the knack of getting on with women. So forgive me if I'm clumsy when I say I get on with you better than I'd ever imagined. I flatter myself we are, in a way, friends.'

'Well,' she relaxed slightly, 'thank you, sir. I think we do understand each other rather better nowadays. It was a bit of skirmish at the outset. I should like to think we *are* friends.' She decided to make things a bit easier for him. 'Now what, as your friend, can I do for you?'

He looked at her rather helplessly, glanced down at his glass and up again.

'You do want me to do something?' she urged. 'Tell me, and I'll do whatever you wish.'

'You don't really mean that,' he hedged. 'You don't know what you're saying.'

'Oh, good gracious!' she said in mock despair. 'I don't mean it literally, of course. If you asked me to jump off a cliff, I wouldn't. But anything reasonable——'

'I *was* going to ask you to jump off a cliff—in a way.'

Her eyes were large brown pools of inquiry. 'What would I be jumping into?' she asked.

'Marriage,' he said, draining his glass. 'I was going to ask you to marry me.'

The brandy was warm and comforting and made her feel slightly whoozy after the sherry.

'Oh, dear!' she said. 'Oh, dear! I mustn't get drunk on top of everything.'

'I thought you were going to pass out, Sister,' Jon said in concern. 'You went so pale, like somebody in shock.'

'I *was* in shock,' she told him. 'The last thing I expected of this little outing was a proposal of marriage. You must be out of your mind. I granted you the hand of friendship, but that's hardly enough, is it?'

'Not usually, I grant you. But I wasn't proposing the usual relationship. I haven't time to go through all the motions, and whoever knows what the end result will be when one does? I think you're a damned good nurse and—I like you, admire your spirit. I think you'd be tolerable to have around and so I had to ask you. You have only to refuse, of course.'

'Of course, and I do so, here and now. You can stop listing my good qualities and somehow making them seem like insults.'

'Insults?' he seemed genuinedly amazed. 'How do you make that out?'

'You make me feel that all you notice is my professionalism, not the woman behind it. Who wants to marry a man who thinks of one as a damned good nurse with spirit? All good nurses have to be spirited or strong-minded doctors would grind them under their heels.'

'Well, that's that,' he shrugged philosophically. 'I hope no harm's been done?'

'No, apart from one small nervous breakdown. Was this why you tried to phone me last week?'

'No. I wanted to talk to somebody about young Simon. I thought you might have been interested.'

'What about young Simon? He's not ill, is he?'

'No.' He grimaced. 'There's not much point in talking about him now that you've turned me down, however. It's my problem.'

'You're very annoying,' she flashed at him. 'Is the problem connected with your outrageous proposal?'

'Entirely. I wouldn't consider getting married for my benefit alone.'

'You wanted to marry so that somebody could look after Simon for you, I gather? Well, what's wrong with a housekeeper, if that's all you want?'

'What's right with a housekeeper? He needs somebody to mother him; somebody young enough to understand kids. He thinks Bob and Kate are his parents, and they want to make it official if he stays with them. Bob has a job in the States to go to, and if they take Simon with them it'll be for keeps. I have to decide if I can offer the boy as good and loving a future as they can. I'm beginning to conclude that I can't.'

'But you're his real father,' Laura said, aghast.

'Yes. To him I'm just another casual caller, however. He wouldn't miss me.'

'But your son—your own son!'

'What can I *do*?' he asked in a kind of helpless desperation.

'You need a wife,' she answered clearly. 'There should be no difficulty. You work in hospitals along with many unattached women, many of whom are probably secretly in love with you and longing for a chance to show it. You have to cultivate the likely ones; you're an attractive man,' she told him frankly.

'*You* obviously don't think so,' he answered grimly, 'and there has to be some feeling on my side for the woman I choose to look after my son.'

She looked at him aghast. 'But you don't love me,' she asserted.

'No. But I've always liked you. That's a new thing for me. From the very first I liked you, I enjoyed our encounters, I looked forward to them. I—I never liked a woman in that way before,' he added rather helplessly. 'It seemed to me rather special, as though trust was involved. But it does all seem rather absurd now. You are right to turn me down so flatly. The whole thing's ridiculous.'

'You do see that?' she asked gently. 'I mean, two people living in the same house with all the trappings of domesticity around them, a child to care for? The emotions are bound to be involved eventually, and then what happens? People are still flesh and blood behind all their efficiency,' she reminded him.

'I had thought of that, too,' he said calmly. 'I looked quite frankly at our respective futures as they seem to be heading. You have been deprived of a great love you feel is unrepeatable; I respect that; you are therefore determined to make your career your life. Other women have chosen to do that, in our profession and others, and some have had it forced upon them. In your own orbit, Ivy Jenkins lost her fiancé in the war and has seemed content to sublimate that side of her nature; she is about fifty and lives alone in a tiny flat. Her life is the night-life of hospital where she is mostly still alone and aloof. How happy she is, nobody knows, but she must obviously carry on until she is superannuated, and then what will be her lot? Claire Martyn is another, though she has lived in the Nurses' Home as long as I can remember. No hospital gossip has ever linked her name with any man. I hear that she and old Saunders are planning to buy a cottage in the town where they can live together. That's fine.

91

They'll be able to talk about hospitals they've known whenever they finish duty and have a home of their own and the security that offers them. But you—I can't see you being content with anything like that. I should hate to see the light in you burn out for want of fuel. You've enjoyed fighting with me—we met as combatants on a common battlefield—and I think this happened because we both had need to feel emotional again, in some way.' As Laura's mouth dropped open, he proceeded, 'It *is* true that those whom we choose as combatants can also be our friends or lovers, as the case may be. One has to be emotionally involved even with one's enemy. It's indifference which has no future. I feel I could have offered you a stimulating relationship, in no way diminishing what you had with Jim, the common interest of a child to bring up and—and maybe, eventually, other children, though that, of course, would all depend on you and—and whether you wanted us to—er—share a room and so forth. Also,' he added quickly, as though thinking he might be shocking her, 'we'd still have our jobs in common.'

'Like Martyn and Saunders,' she added drily, not at all shocked because none of it could be taken seriously. 'If you've thought of so much, how do you suppose I could still do my job *and* look after your child and our children?'

'Ah!' he said triumphantly. 'I see you haven't quite slammed the door in my face. You may have your tongue in your cheek, but I don't think any woman is ever mortally offended by a serious proposal of marriage. I happen to have a colleague married to an ex-sister and she wants part-time employment, afternoons. As a married woman I would suggest you worked from nine until two—we would have a girl, of course, to see to Simon during those hours, and also a daily—then you could spend the rest of the day being a mother, going shopping and cooking the dinner. Weekends, of course, you'd stay home.'

He looked rather startled as she began to laugh outright. It was rather helpless laughter and he saw how her cheeks were deeply dimpled and her eyes rather moist.

'You've certainly got a very workable blueprint, sir,' she said chokily at last, and laughed again as she realised the absurdity of still calling a man 'sir' who had just put such an outrageous proposal to one. It made him appear such a distant stranger. 'I am to work the morning shift in hospital, which Sister X will take over from me because it suits her domestic book to work afternoons, then I am to trip off home to "Mon Repos", or somewhere, where I have a child waiting to call me "Mother" and a husband who will want his dinner, though I don't even know whether he prefers steak to chops, or pork to veal—' she met his eyes and the dimples faded. They assessed each other for a moment in silence.

'—and all the uncertainty of the future, still,' he said eventually, 'only I don't think it would be dull.'

'There's only one thing you haven't thought of, sir,' she said ringingly. 'You have nobody to account to, and so your imagination can run on unfettered. I happen to have a close relationship with a very loving mother and father and a married sister in Australia. How could I say, "I'm marrying a stranger, Mother," and expect her not to have a fit? She would think I'd gone mad.'

'Mothers like their daughters to marry,' he said firmly. 'I'll bet yours is already worrying about your determination to stay solitary.'

'But there are limits,' she expostulated. 'Mum is already matchmaking, but——'

'Think about it,' he said quietly. 'Just think about it. Have dinner with me on Tuesday and tell me yes or no. I won't even mention the subject again if you decide against me O.K.?'

'Oh, it's impossible,' she told him.

'I know, but tell me on Tuesday, eh?'

They were ten minutes late for the dinner, but only Matron seemed to notice their late arrival, as the rest

93

were busily and shrilly still partaking of *aperitifs*. Laura particularly noticed how shrill the Sisters were being, laughing and being familiar with the medical staff in a way which was not encouraged during duty hours. As this was a function to which wives were normally not invited, the doctors and surgeons, the pathologist, hospital secretary and the Board of Governors were, perhaps, letting their hair down, if such can be said of bald-headed men, as many were. Sister Trevor was screaming, 'Oh, Mr Philber, you are a one!' and Sister Martyn was looking absorbedly up into Mr Richmond's face, already quite florid on three gins and bitters, while Sister Saunders animatedly cornered the paediatrician, Dr Ferris, who seemed as though he could neither make her hear nor get away. As she was so obviously dressed up, this evening, in mustard-coloured velvet, she had probably not brought her hearing aid.

Apparently Miss Trueblood thought the preliminaries had gone on long enough, for she spoke to her escort, the Chairman of Governors, and he announced in his plain East Suffolk voice that they might now take their places at table.

There were three tables laid in the adjoining room, in the form of an uncompleted square. At the top table, Matron, her two assistants and the governors sat. On the left sat the surgeons and their registrars with their ward Sisters and a couple of non-resident senior staff, the senior social worker and the X-ray specialist. On the right sat the physsicians with their ward Sisters and registrars, together with the senior physiotherapist and the occupational therapist. On this occasion Jon Warwick was counted among the physicians; he didn't operate at the Cottage Hospital.

As Laura took her place and he sat beside her she felt as though she was still dreaming. This man beside her, with his black thatch of hair and vivid blue eyes, strong, capable hands and general masculine good looks had just put to her a most extraordinary proposal, that they should marry even though they were still practically strangers. He had managed to make the outrageous suggestion sound almost attractive at times, too, but of course, it was quite, quite impossible and she refused to give it any more thought. As she progressed from melon to lemon sole, however, she did not think of other things he had said. She glanced at Saunders, still talking fifty to the dozen to Dr Ferris, and at Martyn, whose tongue had also been loosed, and who was giving whinneying little laughs up at her escort, and she remembered how they really didn't like each other very much, and yet some sort of mutual desperation was driving them to set up home together. Did women need men in their lives so much if they were not to finish up as pathetic oddities? Not all women, of course, became oddities, but elderly spinsters somehow did have a certain look—one could pick them out of a crowd. During Laura's days of probation, confident of their attractions and certain of future conquests, the youngsters would divide their seniors into two groups; those who had had their chances and not taken themm, and those, poor souls, who had never even had a chance.

'I suppose an eighteen-year-old would class me as one who had lost her chances,' Laura silently reasoned, and didn't care for the reasoning and was glad when the waiter removed her plate and brought her back to the present.

'Do you want to be alone?' Jon Warwick asked quietly. 'I don't want to intrude——'

'Oh!' and Laura actually found herself blushing. This man—one's husband? 'No, I don't want to be alone,' she told him frankly, and really enjoyed the next twenty minutes while he told her about the new rehabilitation unit shortly to be opened at Millerdown.

After dessert came the speeches, but though Laura tried to listen and laugh at the somewhat obscure jokes, some magnet in her brain seemed to draw her back to some central theme which was somehow more important than all. A vision recurred to her of a little face, lips sucked in and eyes large and wet and a scarlet flush on each plump cheek; Jon's son, who needed a home and loving parents. Women really didn't need husbands, she thought dreamily, but they should certainly have a child. If all the large families could be distributed so that every woman had a baby, then gone would be all the frustrations and tensions and deprivations peculiar to the single state, though how the unmarried woman would manage to keep herself and the child, without a man behind them, was a bit of a problem.

'I'm not, I *am not* considering this proposal, am I?' she asked herself sharply, as someone at the top table remarked on the service the Founder had done Thornsea by providing the hospital out of his linen-drapery fortune. 'If I changed my mind and wanted to get married, I'm not exactly an old crone, as yet. I'm now twenty-four and have only to socialise more to find a husband of my own choice.'

Jon's hand on her arm brought a peculiar thrill by its unexpectedness. She looked up at him and met the full beam of those eyes, deep with the confidences they had shared and the compliments he had paid her.

'It's all over,' he told her. 'Want to go home?'

'Would you mind?'

'No. I'm tired myself.'

His arm under hers going down the Town Hall steps: 'I've liked you since first I saw you, I enjoyed our encounters, looked forward to them,' she remembered him saying. Well, she liked him, too. If likking was enough then she liked no one better. 'It seemed rather special, as though trust was involved,' well, that was nice to know, too. When you trusted someone—well! what more could you say? 'One has to be emotionally involved, even with one's enemy. It's indifference which has no future.' She could remember it all, like some classic registered in her mind from her schooldays, and wondered if she would ever wish she could forget it. The fact that memory made it seem more important was upsetting. Her mind had not dismissed the absurdity of it, as it should, but was relentlessly considering point and counterpoint as though her future literally was at stake in the decision she made.

In the car she tried to recall how it had been with Jim, but the dominant personality beside her dismissed less physical entities. When she thought of Jim kissing her goodnight it was the imaginary kiss of Jon Warwick's muscular lips which met hers, and his eyes which came into focus drawing away from some secret, magic moment shared.

'We're there, Sister,' his voice came into her wanderings.

'Oh, are we? I must have been dozing.'

Their goodnight handshake was brief because he was wary of touching her and she of being touched.

'Thanks for a lovely evening, sir,' she said conventionally.

'I'm sure you don't mean that, really. You've been in a state of shock most of the time. I should apologise.'

'No. No, don't do that. As you said, no woman is offended by—by—Anyway, goodnight.'

'Goodnight, Laura.'

She turned halfway up the steps to the Nurses' Home as though the sound of her name was a rifle shot. He was still leaning against the car in his dinner clothes, his shirt gleaming, his hands in his trouser pockets.

'I just thought I'd try it out,' he explained.

'That's all right, Jon,' she told him, and as they both turned away from the encounter, smiling, she felt a sudden warmth from understanding what it meant to be liked.

Laura was on duty all weekend and was there to welcome Mrs Kershaw back into the fold.

'My feet are a lot better now, Sister,' she said enthusiastically. 'I may get to walking yet, when you've built me up the way you did before. Mr Warwick said I may have to be content with what's been done. I'm not a good operation risk.'

'That's as well to know,' Laura comforted, somehow lapping up Jon Warwick's opinions as though they were gospel. 'We'll soon get you strong enough to try out your feet.'

It was a pleasant weekend with no crises and Laura often dimpled as she remembered that impossible and yet unforgettable proposal of Jon's. She tried to think of the nice girls in the hospital whom he had possibly never noticed, but she had to admit that niceness wasn't enough. A certain mental agility was necessary to cope with such a man and also a firmness that was entirely feminine in its gentle rigidity. Not every nice girl she could visualise had this silken armour to counter the barbs of the man in one of his stormier moods, nor the resilience to face him again and again in verbal battles he had admitted to enjoying. She could imagine them weeping and inviting his contempt, or being wounded and woeful and quitting after the first unequal round. He *was* a difficult man to marry, she had to agree; but he was also a dangerously attractive one. On the rare occasions he really tried to please one found oneself almost bending over backwards to meet him more than halfway. She found herself trying to imagine him beyond the closed doors of the bridal; well, a girl had to think of such things at times. She couldn't think of him as being brutal and demanding, rather she thought of him as shy, afraid of intruding, having to be encouraged, but once encouraged—! She had to block such thoughts. They made her tingle, and here she was in the cool uniform of her professional efficiency and supposed to be on duty.

'Time for teas, Nurse,' she told the ward junior, whose thoughts had also been far away, though she was supposed to be counting pillow-cases. 'What are the visitors still doing on the ward? Ring the bell now, Nurse, and get on with the buttering. I'll cut the cake as soon as the place is cleared.'

On Monday there was the monthly stocktaking, which kept Laura busy all day. She didn't know why the powers-that-be demanded this monthly accounting of the trivia connected with running a ward. Even the bedpans and bottles had to be counted. Who could imagine anyone dashing away with a bedpan in their suitcase? On the whole she was glad of this extracurricular exercise, for it kept her from fretting about her meeting with Jon Warwick on the morrow. He had seemed rather lost during the morning's round, not at all his lively self, so that she had asked if he had a headache.

'No. Just a bit bothered about everything. You'll understand I'm worried about what to do regarding Simon.'

Of course she understood, and she realized he was anticipating that her answer on the morrow was going to be in the negative. He really couldn't honestly expect anything else. She became a bit bothered, too, and worried for Simon. She wondered if she could offer her services in any other way. Could she take a flat and have Simon with her so that his father would know he was in good hands and visit him regularly?

'By the time I've tied myself down with his child, and he's spending most of his evenings with us, there's no point in not going the whole hog,' she told herself grimly. 'A fat chance we'd both stand of meeting someone else at that rate, and the whole idea is to provide a secure, settled background for the baby. No, I can't see any way out at all. In a way I think I mind, but it's a situation one can't get across to parents like mine. If I could marry Jon in a register office, without having to tell anybody else, I think I'd be tempted to do it. But I must put it all from me in the circumstances. I *must*.'

Then that evening she was called to the telephone by Home Sister.

'Your mother is calling, Sister,' she said.

Laura flew down the stairs fearing the worst. Was Father ill? He had boasted he was growing out of the asthmatic attacks which had plagued him for the past twenty years or so.

'Mum?' she queried. 'What's up? Is it Dad?'

'Oh, Laura, calm down, dear. It's not the end of the world. Your father's fine. Actually it's Jane. She had to go into hospital to save the baby. Guy says she's fairly settled again now, but that she would like us to be with her until the baby's born safely. As you know, Dad and I were planning to go out for a holiday in the summer—their winter, that is—and we see no reason why we shouldn't bring our visit forward if it would reassure Jane to have us there. It is a long way off to be having one's first baby, and she seems to have had a shock thinking she might lose it, so what do you think, Laura?'

'I think you should go if you can manage it, Mum.'

'But you'll have nowhere to go when you have a week-end off.'

'You're joking, Mum! I have married friends galore, *and* Cousin Ethel, whose gingerbread excels even yours.'

'Go on with you! So you don't mind, then, dear?'

'Not at all. I shall be happy to think of you helping to bring my nephew or niece safely into the world. When do you plan to leave?'

'It's a rush, but there're two cancellations on a plane leaving Wednesday evening. We should be with Jane at the weekend.'

'Everything's fitting in splendidly. You're meant to go.'

'And won't you be lonely?'

'Not at all. Mum——?'

'Yes, dear?'

'Actually I have a sort of man-friend again.'

'What do you mean "sort of"?'

'Well, I mean I won't be lonely. I'll be seeing him.'

'And could it be serious?'

'Oh—er—yes, Mum, it could. It could lead to marriage, if that's what you mean. You'd like him, and he's a doctor—an orthopaedic surgeon, actually.'

'Oh, Laura, I'm so thrilled for you! What a pity I can't see him before we leave.'

'It will give things time to develop, dear. You go off to Jane and I'll write every week. Give her my love and a big kiss for you and Dad.'

She was trembling as she replaced the receiver for it appeared that fate had worked on her behalf as it had on her parents', in providing them with seats on a flight for which they might otherwise have had to wait weeks, and so leaving her free to act as she now felt urged to do. On a sudden wave of confidence she decided she would marry Jon Warwick and look after his child for him. Both acts now seemed exciting in prospect and the future beyond would depend on them both as reasonable, mature adults, to give and take and shape as each situation which arose demanded. Her parents could be informed by letter. When they knew about Simon they would realise how urgent the business was and why she couldn't wait for their return. Also she knew she wasn't foolish or headstrong and that whatever she did was done for the best.

'So I've got to learn how to be a good wife and mother,' she decided, 'without having borne the child or fallen in love with the man. It'll be quite a challenge, but I'm sure it can be done in time.'

A day had never dragged since her arrival at Thornsea as that Tuesday did. She heard that Mr Warwick would not be in, but Home Sister had taken a telephone message and a slip of paper rested on the dressing table in her room. 'The Schooner at 8.30. Meet me there,' it said baldly.

'It was a gentleman,' Home Sister had told her, 'but he didn't give his name. He said you'd know it.'

'Yes, I do, thank you, Sister,' Laura assured her.

Obviously Jon couldn't come for her, so she would have to take a taxi, as it was sleeting outside. She always seemed to meet this man outside the hospital to the accompaniment of cold, north-easterly winds. They had blown her to his aid on the bleak cliffs and now they were taking her like tumbleweed to declare herself to be his wife, and she had not yet been three months at the Cottage Hospital.

'But I have known him a long time, really,' she told herself in the taxi. 'I suppose that's because every minute has counted. It's like that with some people.'

This time it was Jon Warwick who grew pale and looked almost faint.

'Well, I'm—I'm jiggered,' was all he said, which wasn't exactly the romantic response Laura had half expected.

It had appeared the subject was never going to be raised, to her, as she toyed her way through a prawn cocktail and then left half of a delicious tournedos steak on her plate. She refused dessert, but Jon was eating cheese and biscuits when he suddenly smiled challengingly and asked, 'Well, Laura? Let's have the final salvo. Sink me without trace and don't bother about a wreath.'

He was smiling all the while, looking quite lighthearted, and she said, 'Well, actually, I've decided to agree. I'll play my part in trying to make a go of it, mostly for Simon's sake at this stage, though I'm sure we won't regret it if we both make up our minds not to.'

It was then the smile faded slowly and his colour went. He looked positively ill as he came out with that 'Well, I'm—I'm jiggered!'

'Had you better get your head down, Jon?' she asked in professional concern. 'You look terrible. I didn't mean to shock you. If you've changed your mind about anything, or got someone to look after Simon, then please don't think any more about it. I'm sorry. Really I am.'

'Laura! Laura!' he begged, and he seized her hand as though dragging himself up from some deeps. 'Don't spoil it by apologising, please. It was all so unexpected that I'm naturally knocked flat, but—but very happy and—and awfully grateful. I haven't anything or anybody else in mind for Simon. I thought I made it clear I can't exchange the good set-up he has for anything less beneficial to him. At present he's young enough to adapt and I, too, am doing what I'm doing chiefly for him, initially. But you won't regret it, Laura, by heaven you won't. I'll be good to you. I think you're—very brave.'

'Oh, Jon,' she laughed weakly, 'I'm not exactly Daniel entering the lions' den.'

'How do you really know?' he asked her, his eyes some- how deep and unfathomable. 'I could be a beast for all you really know of me.'

She swallowed. 'And I could be a harpy,' she coun- tered, 'for all you know. I suppose we both do have a disagreeable side to our natures. We're not angels or we wouldn't be here on earth. We've got to remember that this is one marriage not made in heaven, and to my way of thinking it's like a lift on the ground floor. It can only go up, or stay put. That's up to us. I think it's important we stay friends, rather than try to force a change in our relationship. Some things have to be hurried, but not all.'

'I agree,' he said understandingly. 'Now that I'm coming out of shock I think I'll have a brandy with my coffee. Or is it an occasion for champagne?'

'No,' she said quickly. 'We'll have champagne when we've earned it. Maybe on our first anniversary. You have your brandy and order a Benedictine for me, please.' She crinkled her eyes and shivered. 'Of course I can't help feeling excited,' she admitted.

'Nor I,' he twinkled back at her. 'Now, what about a few snags you mentioned recently? Do I see your father and ask him formally?'

'No, I'd rather you didn't, Jon.' She told him about Jane's threatened miscarriage and her parents' plans to join their elder daughter in Australia.

'They'll be gone at least six months, and as they're flying out tomorrow I think they have enough on their minds at the moment. But I did hint to Mother about you, told her I was seeing you, etcetera, and when she knew what you were she was delighted. Mothers!' she smiled helplessly.

'God bless 'em!' Jon said from the heart. 'Well, there's rather a lot to arrange, as you'll appreciate.'

'How long before we have to take Simon back?'

'Less than three weeks. In that time I have to find a house—my flat's too small, and we must have a girl living in—get married and—' he paused and the next came out with a rush—'I think we'll be expected to take a honeymoon. I don't intend anybody else should know this is only an arrangement of convenience. That's if you don't mind?'

'No, of course not,' she said quietly. 'How will you cope with it all, Jon?'

'Joyfully,' he said frankly, raising his brandy glass. 'Everything's constructive, you see, and I'm a constructive sort of chap. If you ever want to make me unhappy, knock something down that I've built up.'

'I'm not going into this thing intending that anybody should be unhappy, Jon,' she told him sincerely. 'If it so happened that we simply couldn't make a go of it, having tried our very best, then something would have to be arranged amicably. But if I can't make you happy I'll do my best to see you're contented. I don't take big, important steps without anticipating a success. Most people getting married have an emotional involvement, but we have our intelligence. That must be made to work for us.'

'O.K., Laura. I think this is a partnership better sealed by a handclasp than a kiss, don't you?' She put her little white hand into his large, long-fingered surgeon's grasp, and tingled at the contact. 'Some day there'll be the kissing,' he told her confidently, 'but "till cherry-ripe they cry" I'll be happy to be your friend, *and* your husband.'

The handshake became a hand-holding, and lasted much longer than was strictly necessary to seal the bargain.

CHAPTER FIVE

LAURA drove home rather anxiously in the white Triumph Herald Jon had given her for a wedding present. It was her first day as a married woman part-timer at the Cottage Hospital and she had now left her ward in the capable hands of Sister Groves, who was married to a G.P. in the town and liked to work afternoons. She was a childless woman of thirty-eight and had had long experience of orthopaedic nursing during her professional years in hospital. Somehow all had gone so smoothly that Laura couldn't quite believe it; couldn't believe that she was a married woman going home to the large, detached house near the golf-course, to her child and her pleasant domestic chores.

The house was white and was named The Arbor. As she put the car away in the garage she saw Harris, the gardener, busy in the warm greenhouse putting little plants in little pots, and thrilled to think that come summer she would see those same plants probably blazing in full flower in the beds, at present frozen into immobility.

Jon had been lucky to get this house, and completely furnished. Its owners had been about to emigrate and have the furniture auctioned, but for the convenience of moving into a ready-made home, Jon had bought the lot at a ceiling price it probably wouldn't have fetched in auction. There were some items they took a dislike to on sight. The green fitted carpet in the hall was a bit sickening, but Jon had discovered quite good parquet underneath and so, in time, up would come the fitted carpet and down would go a valuable Tabriz rescued from his previous flat on the polished blocks.

It would take time to get things organized the way

they wanted, but time was something they now had. The rush was over and after a necessary period of relaxation and adjustment they could learn to live and do things together.

The nursemaid, Cathy, an orphan, was glad to see her.

'Oh, Mrs Warwick, he's been an angel, so he has. But he's getting a bit restless now, I think he's looking for you.'

Laura entered the nursery with her heart in her mouth, wondering, and from the playpen Simon looked up from bashing one brick against another and his wet face broke into a smile of uninhibited delight.

'Mom-mom-mom-mom——!' he cried out, and she swept him up into her arms and smothered his face with kisses, making unintelligible noises to him in return. This was one love affair which was certainly proving itself very quickly. For the past week, the week following the honeymoon, she had been left to get herself acquainted with Jon's son, and for two agonizing days he had cried inconsolably, fighting her, fighting Jon, fighting Cathy, and only falling into exhausted sleep to recoup enough strength to start all over again. It was the daily, Mrs Gee, who had offered sound advice.

'Let 'im see you, mum,' she had said, 'but don't 'andle 'im too much. 'E 'as ter come round in 'is own time, bless 'is little heart.'

On the third day Laura had crept into the nursery and tried not to look too eagerly at the child in the playpen, whose mouth had already turned down upon seeing her. She had brought a bag of her belongings, hastily packed up when she vacated her room at the hospital, to sort through while Cathy washed the baby's smalls. She sat on the window seat, where the light was good, and pulled her brush and mirror set from the holdall. So that's where they were. She had had to buy a new brush and mirror to take away with her. Next she unpacked a teddy bear nightdress case, which she had been given some years ago, when she first started nursing. A little voice came from the playpen 'Ooh! Ooh!' it urged.

Laura looked up, smiled, and set the furry thing down on the floor with the other things.

'Na, na, na!' Simon said, shaking the rails of his playpen. 'Ah!' he said as she looked at him, and pointed to the nightdress case. 'Wan',' he said quite clearly.

'You want it, Simon?' she asked brightly. 'You want Mummy's teddy?'

The child looked around as though expecting someone else to be present, but already his baby memory was rejecting the past, and, fortunately, Bob and Katie Barnes had kept faith in not coming near during this difficult period of transition.

'Here you are.'

He took the article and squatted at the farther side of the pen with it, giving it an investigatory gnaw and then putting its softness to his cheek.

'Do you like Mummy's teddy, Simon?' Laura was now squatting in the pen herself. 'Look!' she invited, and deliberately glanced down as she saw his mouth pout when she took the article from him. She showed him how to stuff a rubber duck inside the pouch, and a couple of bricks, and thrilled to hear the gurgle of laughter as she produced these again. After that he sat contentedly on her lap and they stuffed and unstuffed the case with toys until he began to rub his eyes with tiredness.

The next time he saw her he didn't cry, but said quite clearly 'Wan', wan',' and the game started all over again. Next day he was saying 'Wan' Mom Mom,' which delighted her, and he began to cling to her skirt and pull himself up into her lap for a cuddle. Jon was obviously pleased by her triumph, and didn't seem to mind that he was apparently still regarded as a stranger in his son's life. A baby needed a mother, and that was really important in these early days.

On the first day back at work, Laura had been worried in case the baby forgot her again. Now she was reassured, however, and could leave on the morrow for her part-time occupation with an easier mind. So adaptable were children that he would soon learn there was a time he must spend with Cathy. She looked forward to the time he would greet his busy father with a joyous 'Dad! Dad! Dad!' and then they would truly have won this initial battle, the reason for all their hasting to the wedding.

After she had played with the baby for an hour it was time for his airing, so she dressed him up warmly, popped him in his pram with his Donald Duck hot water bottle comfortingly beside him and pushed the pram down the long drive and into the nearby park. She loved these outings, sharing a fellow-feeling with other mothers pushing their prams and each thinking their baby was the prettiest, though, of course, Simon was, indisputably. He eventually settled back of his own accord and watched the winter sky through glazing eyes until he eventually slept. She knew, however, even so early in their acquaintance, that if the pram stopped he would wake up like a shot, and so she kept pushing. As she pushed she recalled the immediate past in a clarity of detail which never failed to fascinate.

Miss Trueblood, the Matron of the Cottage Hospital, had been delighted by the news.

'You sly pusses,' she told Jon and Laura. 'I usually spot these things, but I never suspected.'

She told the staff at supper that evening.

'Oh, I do so like weddings!' Mahmoud sighed happily.

'Isn't it a bit sudden?' Martyn had asked sharply. 'Anyway, congratulations!'

'Are you having the baby?' asked the usually quiet Jenkins.

'Of course.'

'Oh, that's good! I'm very glad for you both.'

Sister Trevor had said not a word. She had stayed late because Matron had said there was to be an announcement, but she left pointedly at the end of it.

Then the wedding day itself, bitterly cold and frosty. Laura was sure her nose was blue and felt peculiarly depresssed. The car was sleek and chauffeured which called to take her to the registrar's office, and there Jon was waiting, looking as though he hadn't slept all night.

'Well,' he said, and forced a smile.

'I'm sure we can quite legitimately claim cold feet at this moment?' Laura ventured, and bit her lip which trembled slightly.

'Shall we—' Jon nodded towards a closed glass-panelled door ahead of them—'go in?'

'Of course,' she told him clearly. 'That's what we're here for.'

They had forgotten about witnesses, but the Registrar was prepared. He sent for a couple of clerks from the Public Works department and the ceremony proceeded normally.

Laura hadn't realised how important the words of any marriage ceremony sounded to the people actually getting married, but their responses were firm and they listened to the Registrar's little homily on the responsibilities they were undertaking as though it came from the lips of Socrates. Afterwards, when they had signed the register and been declared legally man and wife, they were able to laugh at one of the Registrar's jokes about a wedding which had started more shakily than their own in this very office. They felt much better, now, even light-hearted. Jon took her to see their new home.

'I kept everybody on—the gardener and the woman who comes in to clean. She has the keys and will keep it aired. She was talking to me about beds—' Jon deliberately looked away as he said this—'I told her to always keep a single bed in the dressing room, furnished and ready, as I was sometimes called out at night and wouldn't want to disturb you.'

'That was very thoughtful of you,' Laura said gratefully, 'and it also happens to be true.'

'I got a nice nursery nurse for Simon,' Jon went on. 'She has gone to get to know him, with Katie's permission, so that he doesn't move into a houseful of strangers.'

'Don't call yourself a stranger,' Laura said quickly. 'Remember you're his father.'

'Well,' he said, when they had looked all over the house and decided they could live with the pea-green hall carpet only so long as it took to take it up, 'we'd better be going.'

'Going?' questioned Laura. 'Where?'

'We're going away for a week,' he said clearly. 'It'll do us both good after all the rush. I would as soon just settle in here, as I expect you would, but I don't think I could stand Mrs Gee's tact, knowing us to be newly married. It's best if we get right away for a bit. As it's such a rotten time of year I've booked us in at a hotel in Jersey. It's supposed to be warmer there.'

She remembered, with amusement, Jon's embarrassment when they arrived at the hotel and he signed the register for them both.

'Oh, sir,' said the clerk in reception, 'there seems to have been a mistake. I thought you booked two rooms, but of course, you must have meant a twin-bedded room. Sorry, sir!—That can be rectified.'

'Oh, if you've kept two rooms, that'll do,' Jon said airily.

'Oh, no, sir. I'm sure you and your wife would rather be together. No trouble at all.'

'But——' Jon was arguing.

'Twin beds will be fine,' Laura interrupted, giving Jon a very direct look. 'There must have been a mistake, as you say,' she assured the clerk.

In the bedroom, overlooking the grey winter waters of the Channel, with the twin beds separated by a yard of white rug, Jon said, rather helplessly, 'I was trying to spare you this, Laura. I was quite prepared to say we occupied separate rooms because I snored.'

'What kind of wife would that make me?' she asked mock-indignantly. 'I'm twenty-four years old and I've already dismissed my husband from me because he snores? At my age I shouldn't care if he stands on his head and practises Yoga. You don't, do you? Snore, I mean.'

'I haven't been accused of that,' he smiled. 'Now it's my turn. Are you really twenty-four?'

'I know I look much older,' she sighed.

'Not you. You act much older. You're just a kid, really, Mrs Warwick.'

She looked over her shoulder sharply, laughed and said, 'I suppose I'll get used to that by degrees.'

'Shall we go for a walk before dinner?' he asked her.

'Yes, if you like.'

It was almost balmy out of doors and they walked companionably for an hour, linking arms quite naturally. Dinner was good and they had appetite for it, scarcely having eaten anything all day, and there weren't many guests in the hotel. Next week it would fill up for Christmas.

'You go off to bed,' Jon said understandingly at eleven o'clock, when Laura was looking strained with tiredness. 'I'll have a nightcap and then I'll join you.'

She knew that he was really giving her the opportunity of undressing in privacy and getting into bed without embarrassment. When he came up he didn't even put the light on.

'Goodnight, Laura,' he said as he climbed into bed, 'it must have been a heavy day for you, one way and another.'

'No, Jon,' she told him, 'it's been quite a good day. The first of many.'

'Good girl!' he said warmly, 'and Amen to that.'

They explored the island during the days and one wet afternoon they went to a cinema. In the middle of a rather tense drama Laura discovered her hand was in Jon's. She didn't know how it had got there, but now she glanced at Jon, finding him engrossed in the film.

'My husband,' she thought, 'and I'm his wife in name

only. I've been in his power, but he hasn't been demanding. He hasn't even kissed me. I—I wonder if he would like to kiss me?'

Jon's gaze met her own, as though sensing her wandering thoughts.

'Don't you like the film?' he whispered.

'Oh, yes. This is one of James Bond I haven't seen before. I—I need to blow my nose,' she added, wriggling her hand until it came loose. As she replaced her hankie she felt an arm had crept across the back of her seat, and she finally relaxed into its embrace.

'I have to start being a little bit of a wife some time,' she told herself.

She remembered vividly the morning she had awakened with a start after feeling lips butterfly-soft against her own. She pushed hair out of her eyes, gazed blankly up into those very blue eyes which began to twinkle down at her in a more familiar and platonic way.

'I had to try a Prince Charming on you,' Jon explained, 'or you'd have gone on for a hundred years. It's after nine and they've got so sick of waiting for us downstairs they've sent breakfast for two up to our room.'

'Oh, lovely!' said Laura, whose real hunger, at that moment, was for more kisses.

'You'd better be mother and pour,' Jon said.

'Would you—' she asked—'please pass me my robe? It's behind the door.'

Obviously he was in a teasing mood this morning. He took the robe down, held it and said, 'Come on, then, get it.'

She was wearing a white filmy nightdress and hesitated, then decided not to be coy. As she tried to reach the dressing robe, however, Jon dodged and weaved like a bullfighter, and his eyes gleamed with mischief and appreciation of what he saw.

'The coffee's going cold,' she said finally, her hands across her chest. 'Please, Jon, give me my robe.'

'You're little,' he said in a tone of wonder. 'You can't be more than five foot three.'

'Five foot four and a half,' she corrected him.

'And I do like that nightie.'

She blushed and without another word he wrapped the robe round her.

'They must have been feeding me raw meat,' he said with a forced laugh. 'Come on and let's eat.' He was putting jam on his third croissant when he suddenly said, 'I wonder why they really sent breakfast up to us this morning? I wonder what they thought we were up to?'

They did some rock-climbing that day and Laura knew they were really putting a lot of physical effort into everything they did because the energy was there and the natural physical outlets between healthy adults of opposite sexes were denied them by common consent. She was extremely aware of her husband as a physical entity today, however. It might have been that the touch of his lips had been the key to that secret part of her which had lain dormant since Jim's untimely death. This part she had thought to be Jim's province, and though she had never intended denying herself to the man she had taken as her husband, when the time was right and proper for such gestures, she had not imagined herself as an eager participant in such an enterprise, but rather as the cool donor of a specialised gift.

She had felt anything but cool that morning, however, with Jon's blue eyes teasing and his bare chest above his pyjama trousers so blatantly masculine. As she clambered after him among the rocks she knew what was happening. Thrust together as they were by circumstances he had deliberately tried to avoid, such as the sharing of a room, there were natural forces at work in them both which simply had to be subdued if they were to continue to respect each other. If they started being physically over-familiar, when they were practically strangers in so many other ways, then they would be no better than animals put together in the same cage simply to mate, and afterwards to be separated before they got round to clawing each other's eyes out, the need for togetherness having been served.

But how they had to batter themselves to get such things out of their systems! Laura was so tired, with every muscle strained and aching, that she could scarcely make it back to the hotel.

'I'm sorry,' Jon told her sympathetically. 'I know I'm whacked, and I've done quite a bit of rock climbing in my time.'

'Perhaps you'd like to go out alone tomorrow?' Laura suggested, being sensible. 'You don't have to drag me everywhere, slowing you down.'

'No, I wouldn't, unless you want a day on your own. In a funny way I like knowing you're there. Maybe I've been lonely and never realised it.'

Sitting as she was in the otherwise empty bar-parlour of the hotel, a Martini in her hand, her feet throbbing, a tear squeezed out and fell on the back of her hand.

'Laura?' Jon asked, in a voice which sounded torn. 'What is it? Does something hurt? What have I done to you?'

She turned her face up to him laughing, but still crying.

'You've done nothing. It's all right. I was touched, that's all, by what you said, and I suppose I'm stupidly tired and ready to be emotional. I didn't want you to go off on your own, really, but I didn't want to be a tie, either.'

'You're joking. We *are* tied. We did that in cold blood. You said we could only go up. Are we—off the ground yet?'

'I think so. Don't you?'

'My reactions are still those of an individual, whereas I believe most marrieds think as a pair. I've quite enjoyed this week. I frankly thought it would be a bit of an ordeal, in anticipation, but it's been nice knowing you up to now, Mrs Warwick.'

'I concur in everything you say. Maybe we're learning to be a pair.'

They changed and went happily in to dinner and to bed early, where they were both sound asleep by ten-thirty.

Laura was dreaming and became a bit agitated. There was a light and talk of a coronary thrombosis and voices, one of which was Jon's, and then silence and a startled awakening. Laura shot up in the darkened room and panicked a little. Where was she? She remembered the dream and put on the light, looked at the time. It was two a.m. and Jon's bed was empty, and cool. Then it hadn't been a dream. He'd been called out to attend to someone with a coronary thrombosis and she should be with him. Wasn't she a nurse as well as his wife?

She put on her robe and sat agitatedly nibbling her nails. Where was he? What was this feeling of deprivation which beset her at finding his bed empty? What raw emotion flowed so freely in the night that became rigid self-control in the light of day? After an hour she heard a door close and stumbling footsteps coming up the stairs. They stumbled heavily and she heard a sharp, fierce expletive. Coming into the room, Jon was rubbing his stubbed toe and staring at her.

'Laura? Why are you awake at this hour?'

'I wondered—I wondered where you were.' She was unaccountably in his arms and nestling. 'I thought I was dreaming about somebody having a coronary, but it was true, wasn't it? They came for you.'

'Yes. One of the guests,' Jon said in a tight voice. 'I accompanied him to hospital. He's not so bad. Now, Laura——'

'It was funny how I thought I was dreaming and yet I was too troubled to sleep.' Her hand crept over the hardened muscle of his biceps, and travelled up to his neck. As she would have stroked his hair he seized the hand and forced it down to her side.

'I think you should get into bed, young lady, don't you?'

She passed her free hand over her eyes, trembling, now.

'Do you, Jon?'

'Yes, I do. Otherwise that lift may take off and go right through the roof. We don't want to bust up the works just yet, do we?'

She yawned uninhibitedly and seemed to deflate.

'How nice you are, Jon.'

'I know, I'm obviously not long for this wicked world.'

'Oh, don't say that!'

'Why? Would you miss me?'

'Yes, I would. I'm growing used to having you around, too.'

Back from Jersey, the week of Christmas had been taken up with Simon. Jon had been a background figure while his wife and son had their own private tussle, and he knew that this was very difficult for her. The child's howling often had her in tears, too, and yet she persisted, changing the soiled nappies of a creature apparently trying to commit suicide by hurling himself from her lap, and bathing a tense, slippery little seal with a fury of a temper which saw her emerge as wet as he was, and yet she somehow won and the house became home, with a woman graciously awaiting him and a child peacefully asleep in his cot.

Now she had started to do her job again, and it looked as though it was all going to work out well. She had to write her parents, tell them the immensity of her news. Already a telegram baldly stating the facts had been dispatched, but this could only have served to make them curious, and she didn't want them to think there was anything fishy.

'Let's go home to Daddy, darling,' she said to Simon as he awoke and regarded her, his eyes like blue pearls and still dewy with sleep.

She had everything a woman could want, she decided, as she pushed the pram back in the direction of The Arbor. Well—nearly everything, she qualified this. If she had been Simon's real mother then there would have been no lack in her very full and busy life.

CHAPTER SIX

AFTER a month Laura took mental stock of her lot and decided that she must be an ingrate, because she was having a bad attack of dissatisfaction. No man could have been more thoughtful or kinder than was Jon. The florist called regularly with sprays of Mediterranean roses, spring flowers from the Scillies and, once, an orchid in a box from goodness knows where. The accompanying cards carried sentiments which made her tingle: *With gratitude—Jon;* one said, and the next, obviously carefully thought out and penned, *Grown in the fresh air and fragrant as you,* and with the orchid, just two words, *No comparison.* She was pleased with these until a comment of Mrs Gee's made her wonder.

'My word!' she said, admiring the orchid. 'You might be still courting, mum, rather than married. My Tom never said it with flowers, not after'e'd got me. I suppose 'e thought 'e said it all in other ways,' and she tittered naughtily and went off about her business.

Laura hadn't really thought there was a great deal missing from her present well-ordered life until a cleaning woman made her feel suddenly underprivileged. She had to be given flowers and trinkets because the greatest joy between man and woman was still a closed book between her and Jon, and seemed likely to be. She hadn't imagined she would be the one to regret the lack of a physical fusion. She had had initial dreams of having to ask an amorous husband to be patient a little longer, and, being a gentleman, in these dreams he had always gone away casting lingering looks of regret upon her. But the reality was that he seemed to have settled down in the dressing-room, next to the big room where she slept, quite contentedly. He came in and out of the main bedroom unselfconsciously to use the wardrobe, but the lingering, regretful looks upon her person were a myth too. He worked hard and was obviously intent only on getting into bed, or so it seemed to her who hadn't lived at such close quarters with a man before and didn't really understand the creatures all that well.

He seemed to be heartier with her than before their marriage. His voice rang, as though for the benefit of others, 'How are you, my dear? Had a good day? Has Simon behaved? I've brought you this,' and "this" would be a pure silk scarf, or a box of chocolates or a bottle of perfume.

He was almost always wildly enthusiastic about her cooking, too.

'That was marvellous, Laura. I really enjoyed it. *Cordon bleu* into the bargain, eh?' and he gave a sigh of contentment.

'It was only spaghetti bolognese,' she said after one of these outbursts. 'I saw the recipe in a magazine and I don't think there was enough seasoning in it. You're easily pleased, Jon.'

'No. No, I'm not. I suppose it's because it's *home* cooking. I look forward to my dinner all day.'

But she fancied that if she presented him with a T.V. frozen dinner he would still wax enthusiastic about it for her sake, and she hated herself for feeling resentful of the fact. She wanted to please him, but not have to find the way to his heart quite literally through his stomach.

A letter from her mother also rubbed a raw place in her.

Dearest Laura,

We were really knocked flat by the contents of the cable you sent, and could scarcely wait to receive your following letter, which arrived this morning. Well, darling, we're so happy for you, Jon and baby Simon. Your haste in this situation we understand, and I know you must be busy getting your house in order and maybe you're still terribly excited about everything, but your letter read like a diary, as though you felt you couldn't share the important things with us. I know the house must be beautiful, and Simon sounds a duck, but you didn't tell us much about Jon, only how busy he was, so it makes you seem to be married to a stranger. Please write next time from your heart, darling, say what you would if you'd come home to see me. I'm glad you've got a good husband, but I can only get to know him through you, and I want to know how happy you are, and how happy he is, bless you both. Does Jon talk about his first wife? Or am I being indelicately nosey?

Jane and Bill send their love, as does Dad. Everybody's fine only it's so hot here.

Love, Mother

She didn't know why she gave the letter to Jon to read during dinner.

'You want me to read this, Laura?' he questioned her, still holding the airmailed envelope in his hand. 'I mean—well, you don't have to show me your private mail.'

'I thought you'd be interested in my family's reaction to our news,' she told him. 'If I hear from any old discarded lovers I promise not to share those with you.'

He read the letter twice before saying 'Hm,' very thoughtfully. 'I suppose I should write to your people myself. That may make me rather less of a stranger to them.'

'When you're still a comparative stranger to me?' she asked in a thin, high voice, but he was reading again.

'I've never had a letter from you,' he smiled. 'Do you normally write like a diary?'

'No. It's an innovation. I thought I was putting my folk fully in the picture, but trust good old Mum!'

'To do what?'

'To smell out this isn't a normal marriage, I suspect.'

For the first time her cooking failed to captivate him and he left his baked apple charlotte on his plate.

'Laura, what's up!' he asked frankly.

'Nothing's up, silly,' she replied, feeling nervous. 'It's just other people treading on my toes, being more observant than I thought they'd be.'

'People other than your family?'

'Yes. Mrs Gee has been remarking that you seem to be called out every night, seeing that the little bed in the dressing-room has always been slept in.'

'I suppose that would strike her. I must remember to make my bed before I go out.'

'She'd probably still turn the clothes down to see if it's warm,' Laura said acidly, 'if she really suspects.'

'So Mrs Gee can go to hell,' Jon said sharply. 'Our domestic can't be allowed to rule our lives.'

'Then I had to face an inquisition at the hospital today,' Laura went on in a complaining voice. 'Trevor was saying that her husband wanted her to have a baby and how he would probably have his way as he was so passionate. Then she glanced at me and asked if you were a satisfactory lover. I was embarrassed and angry with everybody gaping at me and I said I didn't discuss things like that with other women. Trevor then said perhaps there was nothing to discuss as you hadn't done your duty by Jean for months before she died, and that everybody was saying it was obviously a marriage of convenience because of the baby being dumped on you. I didn't know what to say, and I cried, and Sister Martyn said Trevor should watch her foul tongue, and there was a row and I walked out.'

She was almost crying again as she told it.

'Women can be such bitches,' Jon said from the heart.

There was a sudden rising of heat within her which poured out in words before she could think.

'Is that all you can say? Everybody seems to know our private business, talking about us behind our backs, and you can only say women are bitches? My mother knows, and *she* isn't a bitch.'

'Let's leave your mother out of this. We've surprised her, and all she is asking for is reassurance. But these others don't really *know* anything. They're fishing. We rushed into marriage without the usual preliminaries and they're intrigued. Any doctor is a victim of gossip. One who marries a girl, after knowing her for only three months, without any preliminary announcement, can be safely said to have captured the jackpot on the grapevine. Let them talk—conjecture—what harm does it really do?'

'It does a great deal of harm when it's me they're talking to and getting at!' she shouted, not recognising her own voice. 'Are you such a fool that you can't understand?'

He had grown pale and risen to tower over her, and for a moment she thought he was about to strike her.

'I *don't* understand, Laura,' he said in a kind of cold desperation. 'I don't understand what you want me to do or say. We made a bargain, there was no coercion, and by heaven I've kept my part of it to the letter. You said that whereas other couples had emotions, we had our intelligence, and I expect you to use your intelligence in dealing with gossips and any envious hussies who may beset you. What else do you expect *me* to do?'

'You could spend more time at home, for one thing,' she snapped, the devil in her determined to quarrel.

'Yes, I suppose I could,' he lashed back, 'but I haven't wanted to intrude. I thought you had enough to do coping with the other member of my family.'

That hurt because he said *my* instead of *our*. 'Anyway,' he was obviously pretty fed up with the argument by now, 'what would we do if I did spend more time with you—play two-handed whist?'

Her hand flew out at that and she slapped it hard against his cheek, which glowed a dull red against the lividness of the rest of him. His eyes burned with a cold blue fire and she really hoped he would hit her back. He turned away, however, and out in the hall the telephone shrilled. She was leaning against the table when he looked round the door and said in any stranger's voice, 'I have to go out. Motor-cyclist. Sounds bad.'

She wanted to tell him she was sorry, but words wouldn't come and there was no time to express herself in any other way.

'I could say his name or something. I could just be there to open the garage doors,' she decided, and wrestled with the heavy front door. She hadn't known it was snowing and already drifting quite heavily. Cathy was spending her night off with a friend in the town, so there was no need to worry about her. As Laura struggled into the first coat she could see in the cloakroom cupboard, she heard the Jag quietly cutting a track through the snow and accelerate out on the road. She was too late to make any amends for that first terrible quarrel she had provoked, fuelled, fanned and was now, as surely, regretting.

It felt lonely, now, in the house. Simon was still sleeping soundly, and she was trembling with reaction too much to settle down and read a book or watch television. She had to think, answer to herself for the molehill of discontent which had grown into the active volcano of tonight's episode. None of it was Jon's fault. He had been faithful to the letter of their agreement, as he said. She had tried and tried to make him feel guilty of some nameless crime, accused him of neglect when he had been more than attentive and only kept out of the way while she was having trouble with Simon. It was all as they had planned, quite literally, and yet it was all so damned wrong.

She was relieved by this truthful admission, which popped out of the blackness of her thoughts like the voice of hope from Pandora's box. Of course it was wrong for man and woman to live together as good friends. It was a wrong which nature could swiftly rectify, as witness certain episodes during their week in Jersey. Had the honeymoon period been longer then very swiftly it would have become a true honeymoon. Natural attraction was there, was still here, and it became this horrid Mr Hyde of a thing when it couldn't get out. Since Jersey there just hadn't been time or leisure to get as close again, and maybe Jon thought she really was happier being a mother than a wife, and indulged her, out of gratitude, while working like a dog so that he was too tired to torture himself at night with the thought of her lying cool and unresponsive in the next room.

'That's what Mum read—an unemotional, precise record of events, just as it happened. Oh, Jon, I've probably driven you away when my only desire was to get closer to you!' she cried aloud in anguish.

The hours passed and snow piled against the doors and windows. Laura phoned Millerdown at midnight.

'Excuse me,' she told the night porter, 'I'm Mrs Warwick. There was an accident earlier. Is my husband there still?' She added, 'It's a terrible night and I've heard nothing.'

'Just a moment, Mrs Warwick, I'll enquire.' It seemed a long time waiting while the man inquired. 'Mr Warwick was operating earlier, but he left the hospital about an hour ago.'

'Oh—thank you.'

He could go to any hotel, she told herself. There was no need to return through the snow to a wife who was violent in her childish tantrums, so she might as well get into bed and try to relax. She found she could not stop her ears from pricking and listening, however, even though the snow blanketed most normal sounds there was the howl of the north wind in all the chimneys.

Was that the click of the gate?

It was after one and she threw on a robe and was down the stairs and tugging at the front door. A mass of snow fell in as she pushed her way out, and there, surely enough, was a figure toiling wearily up the drive.

'Laura! What are you doing out here in nightclothes?' His teeth were chattering, she noticed.

'Never mind about me. What happened to you, Jon?'

'The car's in a drift about a mile back. I walked.'

'You're frozen, Jon.'

'Yes, I am pretty cold.'

'I'll make you a hot rum toddy. You go and get und-ressed.'

He was still struggling with buttons, with frozen fingers, when she joined him, and immediately she helped.

'Now get into bed and drink this. The big bed—' she said firmly. 'There's a hot bottle and it's warm from me. Also I want to say I'm sorry for—for everything.'

'I can't stop shivering,' he said apologetically, trying not to touch her.

'You've probably taken a chill. I'm gooing to wrap myself round you. I'm warm as toast.'

'The rum will probably work soon,' he decided.

'You do forgive me, don't you, Jon?'

'For what? You were upset. I would be in your shoes, hearing the Trevors of this world digging their little dag-gers in.'

'I didn't mean to hit you, Jon.'

'Forget it. I rather admired you for it, actually. You really hurt.'

'Can I—kiss it better?'

'It's better, but I'll take the treatment just the same, if you don't mind.'

They kissed, and it was not on the cheek.

'I'm warm now,' Jon said eventually, 'so I'd better get into my own bed.'

'This *is* your bed. It's our bed.'

'Are you saying you want me to stay, Laura?'

'Yes, I am.'

'You know,' he said softly, as he caressed her soft, warm young body, 'that if I stay the lift's going to go up, don't you?'

'I was beginning to think it was out of order,' she sighed contentedly.

Sister Bradfield, as she was still known when on duty at the hospital, positively tripped about on that snowy morning, so that old Mrs Kershaw was moved to remark on it.

'My, Sister, but you do look 'appy!'

'I *am* happy,' answered Laura.

'You know, if you'll pardon me, I couldn't really tell till now that you're a bride, Sister? You've been busy adjusting, I know, but today you look radiant. You're really bonny.'

'Well, thanks!' Laura was rubbing the woman's pressure points. She was due that day to try out her feet, still splinted though they were, and it would be a relief for her to leave the bed, if only for an hour or two.

Laura didn't mind it being noticed how differently she viewed life today. She was happy, and she had made Jon happy. She wouldn't have believed how their coming together could make such a difference, give the wintry world the rosy glow of June suddenly.

'They say it's bad outside,' Mrs Kershaw said conversationally. 'How did you get in to work, Sister?'

'With difficulty,' Laura said, and laughed as she remembered.

'Come on, wife,' Jon had said gaily, 'I've rung up the A.A. and told them where to find my car. They're getting it dug out, but we'd better go along there together, and then I'll give you a lift in. I'm only on duty for the morning, so I'll bring you back home when you finish.'

Though snow-ploughs had cleared the main roads, the snow was deep on the footpaths and, like children, they had snowballed each other as they walked, been utterly uninhibited, and, at one point, rolled together down a bank of snow.

'Decorum, Sister,' Jon said softly as they exchanged meaningful glances before rising again and continuing their walk. 'There's a time and place for everything, unfortunately.'

She had laughed again and, hand in hand, they had hurried to reach the Jag, which a smiling motor patrolman was watching for them. The kiss as they parted, for just a few hours, was as tender as though they had been lovers for many years. She pondered on the purely physical act of human love, marvelling that it could, apparently, warm the heart like this. This morning she felt very tender towards Jon, wanted to live with him and be his true wife for ever and ever. She couldn't imagine any couple, who had married for more sentimental reasons, being more content with their lot than was she and, she hoped, Jon. She couldn't yet read his mind, but she was closer to him, and she would be closer still if goodwill had anything to do with it. She had heard that a man's regard for a woman was always earthier than was hers for him, but no man could have brought her more joy, and with such gentleness, or have made her feel as beautiful in the cold grey light of dawn as she had been when she had been fuel to the fires of desire.

During the coffee break she almost bumped into Eve Trevor, looking somehow nipped with cold.

'I say—Sister.'

'Yes?' Laura could bear no ill-will today. She smiled encouragingly.

'I'm sorry if I upset you yesterday. I frankly didn't know anybody in our profession could be so touchy.'

'Oh, that's all right. You took me by surprise, and I never have been one for girlish confidences.'

'I thought maybe I'd hit the nail on the head——?'

Laura still smiled but didn't answer. Now she was no longer vulnerable.

'The others said I ought to apologise,' Trevor added uncomfortably.

'Oh, think no more about it, Sister. Are you going to coffee?'

'Yes. Has Jon—that is, Mr Warwick, of course—has he ever said anything about me?'

'Oh, yes,' Laura answered quickly, 'on and off he has. You were a great friend of his first wife's, weren't you?'

'I used to pretend to have a crush on him, just to tease Jean. Did he——?' Laura contrived to look blank, so Sister

Trevor giggled and said hastily, 'Anyway, there's never really been anybody for me but my husband, Ron.'

'Of course not,' Laura agreed, as the canteen assistant handed them cups of coffee and a few biscuits.

'Actually I may become a customer of yours before long,' Sister Trevor again confided, quite chummily.

'Really?' Laura asked.

'I'm having trouble with a disc. At the moment I'm wearing a contraption which nearly kills me, but your dear husband thinks a month's bed rest here in hospital might do the trick. He doesn't believe in surgery unless everything else has failed.'

'Have you a lot of pain?' Laura asked sympathetically.

'Mainly when I change position suddenly. At the moment—none. But I could be screaming by tonight.'

'Oh, dear!' Laura said. 'Well, the sooner we have you in, Sister, the better.'

'I'm glad we've had this little chat. I must admit I haven't been very nice to you in the past.'

'Water under the bridge,' Laura smiled, and realised she would soon be seeing Jon again. Happiness radiated from her. 'I'm glad we've had a chat, too. Let's have more of them from time to time, eh?'

'You bet,' Sister Trevor said under her breath, though Laura only saw her brilliant smile as she departed, 'I haven't finished with you and lover-boy yet, not by a long chalk.'

CHAPTER SEVEN

'You didn't tell me you'd written to my parents,' Laura said to Jon as they dined together one evening about a month later. 'What did you say? Go on, tell me!'

'Shan't!' he smiled, reaching for her hand across the table and squeezing it gently.

She thrilled at his touch. Her eyes were beginning to thrill at the sight of him before he could touch her. They were happy together, happier than she had ever thought possible, and this never ceased to surprise her. She had expected to find a mutual contentment as the goal in this adventure of theirs, if it was successful, based on their community of interest, a genuine liking for each other, and the good sense to make the best of a situation. But the best was proving better than she had dared imagine; she greeted each morning, as John stirred beside her, with a surge of wild, exulting happiness, which had to be battened down, but still simmered gently within her all day, like a volcano with the constant promise of eruption in its core. She wondered if it was the same with Jon, or if she was racing ahead of him as the ingenue of the duo. After all, he had married for love, once—*his* love, at any rate. So what were his true feeling for her, who had physically capitulated to him because it seemed morally wrong not to, and who ran his house, looked after his child and did her own job into the bargain?

Was he just extremely grateful and pleasurably surprised?

She wanted him to feel more because—God help her!—she was nervous of the one-way traffic of falling in love with him if she should be performing a solo. He couldn't be nicer. He still sent her bouquets of flowers— they must have cost him a fortune at this time of year—

and insisted on giving her a three-strand necklace of lovely cultured pearls for her birthday, which he had missed all unknowingly as they were still, in so many ways, strangers, and there were many things they didn't know about each other.

In a way these acts were like courtship, though instead of leading up to it they came after the event, which made them even more precious to her.

She had read the latest letter from her mother, earlier, and Mrs Bradfield had seemed completely reassured after her initial doubts.

'*—My dearest, you sound so happy,*' she had written, '*and so does Jon. He wrote to us, though he says he wasn't telling you, and your father and I now know you've got the sort of husband we've dreamed of for you. Your first letter was a bit like the telegram and told us nothing more, but I do understand how hectic it must have been for you and how you must have worried about our reactions. Well, you have our blessing and we now understand why things had to be rushed. I feel I've known Jon for years; he has the power of conveying his personality in a letter. Dad will be writing him separately——*'

'Have you heard from my father yet?' Laura tried again, as she served the dessert.

He caught her round the waist and pulled her down on his lap.

'What a little nosey-parker you are!' he told her as she wriggled. 'I can see if I don't tell you all you'll be steaming open my mail.'

'Oh, Jon, I would never do a thing like that!' she assured him.

'But you want to know what I had to say to your parents, don't you? You're dying of curiosity.'

'I'm just interested,' she admitted, and he squeezed her, met her anxious eyes and became serious.

'Well, first of all I wrote "Dear Mum and Dad," and that brought a thrill all its own. You know the circumstances of my childhood. I never remember writing that before.'

'Poor Jon!' she said quicklyy, and kissed his ear.

'No, fortunate Jon,' he insisted. 'The poor are deprived all their lives. I've landed lucky. As far as I recall I then reassured them as to my means and ability to keep you in the manner accustomed, and so forth. I said you didn't have to do a job, but you wanted to. O.K.? I said I hadn't started beating you yet, but that would no doubt come in due course. . . .'

She tweaked his hair where it curled at the nape.

'I thanked them for their lovely daughter,' he continued seriously, 'and hoped Jane would, in due course, safely produce her child. I then hoped they would co-opt Simon as a member of the family and allow him to think of them as adoptive grandparents in due course. I think that's about all, and no, I haven't yet heard from your father.'

'I think it was very nice of you to write,' Laura said softly. 'Mother is very much happier about everything.'

'Are *you*?' he asked quickly. 'That's what's really important to me.'

'Yes. Yes, I am,' she said frankly, getting up from his lap. She wished he had said, 'So am I,' but he tucked into his dessert without giving her the peculiar satisfaction she would have gained from such knowledge.

Another month passed and there were developments at the hospital, practically none at home, but that was all to the good, because at home, Mr and Mrs Jon Warwick were well and truly content with their lot and one another. Their domestic course was set fair and the atmosphere untroubled. They had frankly discussed the subject which, a couple of months ago, would only have embarrassed them, the possibility of Laura's becoming pregnant.

'Well, I'm not, up to now,' she told Jon.

'You can be sure?'

'Oh, yes, I'm sure.'

'I'm equally sure that's not thanks to either of us,' Jon said with a wry grin. 'But now we've had this bonus, Laura, what do you think about starting our own family?'

She considered. They had made love regularly and taken no precautions. Supposing she couldn't——? This was an unbearable thought and she thrust it away. She would be so happy to bear Jon's child, but he always considered her and left the major decision of their relationship to her. This left her in a certain amount of doubt as to his desires, other than that of wanting to please her.

'I think not yet,' she said thoughtfully, 'while Simon's so little. He's had one big shake-up and a new baby might be more than he can take.'

'Right-ho,' he said agreeably. 'You'd better go and see Mary Pettit pretty quickly. Until you give me the "all clear" I'd better, with profound regret, betake myself to my dressing-room.'

Dr Pettit was the local Family Planning Officer, who held a clinic at the Cottage Hospital each week. Laura decided to see her privately. She didn't want Jon to go back to sleeping alone, either. Within a few days, just as Mrs Gee was beginning to lift a quizzical eyebrow again, they were back together, however, and, if possible, even more joyously than before.

At the hospital the young husband in the spinal bed, Roger, died, much to everyone's relief apart from his younng wife, who had always believed that if she sat beside him long enough he would one day open his eyes and recognise her. She couldn't be made to believe that even if the eyes did open there would no longer be intelligence shining in them, but Laura understood how hope must burn eternally in the human breast or we would none of us, at times, be able to carry on.

'It's as though life's over,' the poor girl grieved, as Laura gave her a cup of tea, laced with brandy, in her office. 'I can't go on without Roger. I dunno what to do.'

'Believe me, time heals,' Laura said soothingly.

'Oh, they all say that, don't they? Them what don't know what they're talking about, that is.'

'I know what I'm talking about,' Laura insisted.

'But you're married to Dr Warwick. He ain't dead as a doornail, like my Rog.' Tears poured through the girl's thick fingers, which Laura was glad to see. There was always healing in tears.

'No, he isn't, thank God!' she said from the heart. 'Less than a year ago I sat in hospital, like you, watching my fiancé die a little more every day of an incurable disease. I thought I would never get over it, and at first it is pretty bad, and other people try to understand, so don't thrust them away. But I'm a living proof that one does recover. I'm married to Dr Warwick, as you say.' The other still wept, but she was listening as she sniffed.

'No kidding?' she asked wetly.

'No, my dear, no kidding. It won't be easy, but it'll get easier. You'll be eager to live again and you're young. I think your mother's here now. I'd like a little talk with her.'

'O.K., Sister, I'll wait outside. I never knew you'd been through it, too. You've done me a lot of good, you 'ave.'

Jim Potts, who had been in the Cottage Hospital since Laura's arrival, suffering from progressive infective arthritis of the right knee, was discharged, walking quite confidently on crutches, on the same day Sister Eve Trevor was admitted to a private staff side-ward on complete bed rest. Any hospital is always indulgent to its own sick. Sister Trevor, lying flat on bed-boards, had her personal discomfort minimised by a preponderance of visitors. She was also coaxed to eat tasty snacks for her enjoyment, and so, unhesitatingly, dismissed the plainer, stodgier hospital fare. The room was like a florists' shop. When Sister Trevor had no visitors she was rather heavy on the bell, summoning attention. Laura, who seemed to be eternally short-staffed, appeared to spend most of her morning attending to her colleague and she tried to be magnanimous about it, because they had once not been friends.

She was thankfully catching up on charts when Jon arrived, and for once she was not glad to see him, thinking it meant a full round, for which she wasn't prepared.

'It's all right,' Jon assured her. 'I've only come to see Sister Trevor.'

'Oh. I believe she has a visitor.'

'Well, I'll ask the visitor to push off for five minutes. Don't bother coming, my love. I feel, together, we inhibit her.'

Laura wondered what he meant by that. She always found Eve Trevor anything but inhibited.

She settled to her chart-filling and looked up in soome irritation as a tap came on the partly-open door.

'Yes?' she called, thinking it to be one of the staff, but it was a man who looked in on her, a good-looking tall man with fair, wavy hair and tawny eyes, together with a cheerfully lascivious grin.

'Yes?' Laura asked again. 'Did you want something?'

'Ba-bee!' came the response. 'That's what I call a leading question. What I *want* and what I *get* are different sides of the buttie, as they say where I come from.'

Laura flushed and indicated the work on her desk. 'As you see, I'm rather busy. Do you want to see someone?'

'I *was* seeing someone, darling, when I was kicked out on my ear. I used to slave here, the name's Falconer,' and he held out a hand she could scarcely ignore. '*Dr* Falconer.'

Falconer? Falconer? She pondered. The name only tinkled a distant bell, however.

'You are Sister Trevor's visitor?' she asked.

'Yes. The poor darling's quite a wreck, isn't she?'

'Oh, I'm sure we'll get her right in time,' Laura felt bound to say.

'Your name——?' he asked with a smile. 'You're new since my time.'

'Oh, yes. Sorry! Laura Bradfield,' she said unthinkingly.

He was still holding her hand and she pulled this away rather pointedly.

'I'm a devil for holding hands with pretty girls,' he admitted. 'Some men gamble, others drink, but I hold hands—for starters, that is.'

Laura smiled at last.

'Now that's better,' grinned Dr Falconer. 'I was beginning to think I wasn't going to get anywhere with you. Dinner this evening?'

Laura's eyes opened wide.

'Dr Falconer, you're obviously no end of a success with most women, but I'm going to put you out of your misery very quickly. Nothing doing.'

'Well,' he shrugged amiably, 'I call that a straight answer to a straight question. Actually there's not much local talent left hereabouts. When I was here before there was Eve, and Jean, both lovelies like yourself. Now Eve's married some idiot and Jean's dead.'

'You mean Sister Yorke?' Laura asked. 'You knew her?'

'*Knew* her?' the other echoed. 'We were like that.' He held up two fingers entwined. 'Unfortunately my wife didn't understand and threatened a stink, so I had to do a disappearing trick.'

Laura said, looking pale and shocked, 'I don't think you should tell all this to a stranger, Dr Falconer.'

'A stranger?' he echoed. 'You're one of us, aren't you? I wanted Jean to come out into the open and help me get a divorce, but she wouldn't hear of it. Instead she kicked me in the teeth by marrying Warwick. He and I never did get on. She couldn't have thought of anything worse to hit me with. I don't think he was any too happy to see me just now, either. They say he's now made a marriage of pure convenience, the rotter!'

Laura was now very pale and tense.

'I think I ought to inform you, Dr Falconer, that I am Jon Warwick's wife.'

He had the grace to blush. 'Oh, I say, I'm sorry! How

was I to know? Why are you using an alias?'

'Because I'm known on my ward by my maiden name.'

'Well, I've said nothing against Warwick, have I? Only that we both fancied the same woman, and he got her? I—I, suppose it would be as well if I shut my big mouth, eh?'

'Yes, it would, if you don't mind.'

'Just tell me—how's the kid?'

'What kid?' asked Laura.

'There was a child,' the other said patiently, 'I got the job of getting him started in life. I have more than a passing interest in that boy.'

'Simon's very well,' Laura said flatly, 'and now, Dr Falconer. . . .'

She saw Jon's large frame in the doorway and watched the two men's eyes lock as in a wrestling hold.

'Don't you work any more, Falconer?' asked Jon at last. 'Mornings are our busy times.'

'Are they now? Yes, I do work, I'm in general practice locally. But I have a day off and thought I would look up an old friend or two. I won't keep you——' he nodded in Laura's direction, gave Jon another look and departed.

'I don't want that chap in here again, do you hear?' Jon asked fiercely after shutting the door.

'Jon, this is my office,' she said reasonably. 'I can't——'

'Your office on *my ward*,' he suddenly blasted at her, so that she quailed, not believing he had spoken to her in such a tone.

'I was about to say,' she said in a thin, shaken voice, 'that I can't bar anyone who asks to see me. Dr Falconer was a visitor and——'

'Look, Laura, I'm sorry.' He put a hand to his eyes. 'He has that effect on me. I'm sorry. It was unreasonable. Forgive me?'

'Oh, Jon!' she didn't know what to say. The man who was her husband, in whose arms she had lain in rapturous embrace, had a few seconds ago reverted to a coldly furious and terrifying stranger. He was still there between them, keeping them from getting close again.

'I have to go now, Laura,' Jon said at length, and tried to joke. 'Don't worry, it may never happen.'

But while she forced herself to smile back she felt that it already had happened and she *was* worried. The past had intruded into the pleasantness of the present, like the serpent into Eden. Would things ever be quite so wonderful again?

Eve Trevor lay, supine and very beautiful, on the hard unyielding bed. She was the last patient Laura visited before leaving for home on that rather upsetting morning, and for once she was alone.

'Hello, Sister!' she greeted formally, opening her green eyes very wide. 'I was just thinking of having forty winks. I get so bored and my heels are tender.'

'Staff Nurse will be doing your pressure-points in a few minutes. I'm surprised you're bored,' Laura added brightly, 'I would have thought you'd be glad of a few minutes to yourself.'

'Oh, all those callers, you mean? I get fed up of shop talk, but it does help to pass the time.' She lowered her eyes and regarded her pink nails for a second. 'I was glad to make things up with Jon. He was very sweet. It was just like old times again. Thanks for letting him come by himself.'

Laura forbore to say that she hadn't been given any choice. The bitterness of gall was once again in her mouth.

'Are you upset?' Eve Trevor asked suddenly.

'What about?'

'Well, I don't know. Perhaps you minded me asking Jon to come and see me. You look upset.'

'I'm tired, Sister. I seem to do a day's work in half a day, somehow.'

'I know. We're the most overworked profession in the country. What do you think of Miles Falconer?'

'He talks too much.'

'I know. He told me how he was doing a sort of confessional when you suddenly said you were married to Jon. Actually he was quite upset. I think he fancies you.'

'Sister Trevor!' Laura protested.

'No, I mean it. His marriage was disastrous—she was old enough to be his mother—and he has been looking for his ideal woman ever since. He's free now, of course, and hunting like mad. I'm telling you, he likes you.'

'Too bad,' Laura decided, turning to the door. 'I'll remind Staff Nurse you'd like a rub. See you tomorrow.'

'How'm I doing?' Eve Trevor asked the ceiling when she was alone once more. 'It's like playing chess with live pieces. I can hardly wait to tell dear Jon that his old rival has an eye for his new wife, as well as the old, and that she didn't exactly repulse him.'

It was fortunate that an emergency kept Jon late at Millerdown for that afternoon had dragged for Laura, who kept remembering that scene in her office and was surprised how each time the remembrance hurt anew. There wasn't only the hurt but a kind of anger, too, which demanded, 'How dare he speak like that to me!'

Simon seemed to sense her aggrieved mood and was quite naughty. As she was getting him ready for their walk he threw a toy brick at her, and as it caught her on the cheek it hurt and made her want to cry.

'Oh, Simon!' she cried out, and as he stared at her she realised it was nobody's fault but her own. Children and animals liked an unchanging pattern, for people and things always to be the same. She had come home as much a stranger to the child as Jon had become, in one awful moment, to her, and he was only showing how upset he was in the one way he knew. 'Darling!' she suddenly swept him into her arms, battening down her unhappiness. It was a temporary thing, it *had* to be.

But as she waited to serve the dinner, the expensive T-bone steaks done to a frazzle, resentment mounted in her so that when Jon opened the door with his own key she was awaiting him.

'Can't you remember to phone when you're going to be late?' she demanded. 'Am I expected to read your mind and put a dinner on the table that's fit to eat at any hour you choose to turn up?'

He was now seeing her as she had seen him, as a cold-eyed stranger.

'Excuse me, must be the wrong house,' he said politely. 'I'll go out and come in again.'

'Hello, Laura!' he said heartily, the second time. 'I'm sorry I'm late, but I had to go out to a multiple crash. There were so many broken heads and battered bodies that I forgot to phone.'

She had crumpled in the moment he had turned and left, however.

'Oh, Jon, I'm sorry. I must have sounded like a harpy. I should know what it's like being a doctor's wife, shouldn't I? I see both ends of the stick. I—I have a headache, too,' she fibbed.

'Go off to bed early with a couple of aspirins. Is dinner quite ruined?'

'Well, I know you like your steak rare, but it got rather crisp as time went by. Actually it must be charcoal now. I just remembered I forgot to turn off the grill.'

He settled for soup and a ham sandwich and they decided to retire early. In fact Jon was asleep by the time she had emerged from her shower and it was not consideration made her slip away and creep into the bed in the dressing-room. It was pure, unadulterated pique that he could sleep while she was feeling so hurt and neglected.

She opened her eyes and saw Jon looking down at her. It was still dark and she guessed it was betweeen two and three a.m. She thought she had only been asleep a few minutes.

'What's up, Laura? Head bad?'

'No. I——'

'Then what's up? Was it me flying off the handle like I did?'

'That and—other things.'

'Look, love, I wasn't mad at you, I was mad at him.'

'But you shouted at me.'

'I know. If I'd shouted at Falconer it would have been a brawl, but you're my wife. It was like a safety valve. You understand?'

'No, not really.'

'Come on, let's make it better.' He slid into the small bed beside her. 'Now it's you who's cold. You remember that first time?'

She remembered, but this was the first time she had had to pretend to enjoy his lovemaking, because she knew Jon wouldn't touch her unless he thought she was with him all the way.

CHAPTER EIGHT

THE weeks slipped away and spring came to Thornsea, though winter's chill remained in the persistence of the north-easterly wind which cut through the lengthening sunny days almost without cease. There was the same sort of chill wind blowing through the marriage of Jon and Laura, those good friends who had decided friendship and intelligence were sufficient basis for the closest of all ties between a man and a woman, and were now wondering. There was nothing on which Laura could actually lay a finger, but though apparently intangible it was as wide as a house and as insidiously harmful as water leaking from a hidden pipe and rotting the very foundations of a well-built house.

Jon hadn't raised his voice to her again, but now she felt bitterly about the fact that he was almost too polite to her, at all times, so that she felt more like a Lady Mayoress than his wife. Though they still occupied the same bed there was no longer intimacy between them. While she was still upset from that row she had tried to make all come right in the way which could bring them closest, but he had been polite about that, too.

'Look, Laura, my sweet, you don't have to force yourself, you know. I'm not an animal. I can wait until you're in the mood.'

She thought grimly to herself that he was too damned self-controlled to live. Didn't he see that if they lost *that* part of their life together there was nothing left? Well, she was damned if she would cheapen herself to make the effort again, without encouragement. She didn't see consideration in his words, only rejection, and, having started, it seemed that they stung each other continually, as though they were a hive of bees, and, almost too deliberately, neither showed that they were hurt or offended.

Perhaps there really was nothing to see of the deterioration, Laura pondered; because neither Mrs Gee nor Cathy seemed to sense anything amiss.

'Possibly the whole thing's in my mind,' she suggested to herself, in a kind of deliberate self-torment. 'If I was the only one to put anything into this marriage, I'm possibly the only one to miss it. Maybe Jon hasn't even noticed the change in us, or even the channge in me. He's not in love with me, as he was with Jean. But then I'm not, and never have been——' she drew back from saying more and regarded herself, wide-eyed, in the mirror. 'Can I have fallen in love with him?' she asked herself. 'Is that why I shrink up like a sensitive plant whenever he's near, nowadays? I suppose I'm the one to have broken the rules and so deserve all I get.'

It was true that Laura's heart had awakened more readily to love than she had imagined possible, it was because she had considered herself immune that she had undertaken this venture, hoping only to be interested, but not emotionally involved. But the intention and the reality were by no means aligned, as she was discovering.

'How awful if he suspects how I feel and knows he can't respond in the same way!' she pondered. 'It wasn't intended to be a love match. Maybe my reactions have embarrassed him and now he doesn't even find me desirable.'

There were so many possibilities, however, that she couldn't name them all. She went about her various duties like an automaton, trying to believe that if she didn't probe too deeply into anything, all might soon come to rights of its own accord. She thought Jon was thinking along these lines, too, when he talked to her one evening.

'Look, Laura, there's something I have to discuss with you. . . .'

'Yes?' she asked, immediately on her guard, her heart

leaping uneasily in her chest.

'It's about holidays. Are we going away together this year?'

She swallowed the lump in her throat. What sort of a question was that coming from a husband?

'You ask as though there's an alternative,' she said rather acidly.

'Well, of course there are alternatives,' he said grimly, 'if we're looking for them. Look, Laura,' he said more gently, 'you may be regretting the drastic step we took, and I for asking you to take it, but isn't it early days for chucking in our hands? I—' he shrugged his shoulders helplessly—'I don't frankly know how to get you out of this mess.'

Because she loved him, she felt for him more than herself.

'I don't recall asking to be got out of anything,' she said in a thin, high voice she scarcely recognised as her own.

He looked at her sharply.

'You mean you think there's a chance for us?' he asked.

'I'm prepared to make the best of——'

'A bad job?' he queried wryly.

'No, I wasn't going to say that. I was going to say, of what we've got. Also, I'm sorry I seem to have disappointed you.'

'No, you haven't done that, Laura. I've had more out of living with you than I expected, and I'm grateful.'

'You're speaking in the past tense.'

'The present is only ever now, this very minute, and I'm trying to say let's be friends.'

'I'm willing,' she said, and held out her hand, which he took and held for a moment in his own, looking happier.

That's it, she told herself. He only really offered friendship, in the first place, and I pushed in so close to him he couldn't understand my demands on him. I've got to take what he offers and on his terms. 'You wanted to discuss holidays,' she reminded him. 'I'll go with you, of course, if you want me to. So long as you do what you want to, even if it's fishing, or duck-shooting. Simon and I will occupy ourselves quite happily.'

'If we're taking Simon we'll take Cathy. I have the offer of a summer cottage near Bideford. You and I can do some sailing. Have you ever . . .?'

'No, but I'm quite willing to learn.'

'Good girl! I'm glad we've had this chat, aren't you? I suppose we didn't reckon our lift visiting the basement occasionally, but of course all the best lifts must do that to take on new stock.'

'That's true,' she smiled.

'You know you're free to have any friends you choose,' he next said.

'Yes, I know,' she readily agreed, not quite knowing what he was talking about.

'Whether I like them or not,' he proceeded.

She just looked at him, pondering he couldn't dislike any of her friends seeing that he had never met them.

'I'll bring the coffee in,' she said in a wifely tone, and smiled to show that she hadn't forgotten the conciliatory nature of their conversation. It did seem that he really had been in a fog as to the cause of their apparent differences, but she wouldn't make the same mistake again of asking him more than he was prepared to give.

That night he turned to her, after they had said good-night, and kissed her in a way that was a question. She answered in the same manner with her lips, and once more they came together, fully and passionately, and were one. But it was as two they parted and thought their own thoughts.

'I'm surprised we can—without love,' Laura pondered as sleep waited to enfold her, 'but I'd rather Jon wanted me physically than not at all.'

Eve Trevor had left the hospital after her month's bed-rest and took two weeks' sick-leave. She returned to duty as bright as a button looking rested and tanned and very pretty.

'Ron took me to Jersey, to a honeymoon hotel,' she told her colleagues with a laugh. 'Jon Warwick gave me the address. It's where he took you,' she told Laura. 'Naturally I asked the staff if they'd kept tabs on you.' Laura flushed darkly. 'It appears Jon booked separate rooms, by mistake,' she looked round in joyous anticipation. 'Imagine! Separate rooms on a honeymoon!' She hooted with laughter and Laura decided to smile too, before she could collapse in tears of mortification.

'The mistake was quickly rectified,' she volunteered, 'as no doubt you have been told, Sister, by your spies. Anyway, you look a lot better for your holiday.'

'Not holiday, sick-leave. I have my holiday yet to come. We may go to Majorca this year.'

'Lucky!' said Jepson. 'Bridlington is my lot. But after all, I have had my share of the sun in my time.' She laughed her big calypso laugh and the others joined in. There was a general discussion about holiday plans and Laura was asked where she was going.

She felt nervous of letting Trevor know of their plans. Maybe Trevor was capable of turning up in Bideford and spying on them there.

'Nothing's really decided yet,' she temporised.

'You have to book early or you can't get in anywhere,' said Sister Mahmoud.

'I thought Jon told me he'd taken the offer of Mr Richmond's Devon cottage,' said Eve Trevor ringingly. 'Fancy him not letting you know.'

'Oh, he did mention it,' Laura said hastily.

'I wonder!' Trevor said mischievously. 'Maybe he was hoping to sneak off down there and do some remembering. After all, he did take Jean to the cottage. Oh, me and my big mouth!' she exclaimed as everyone stared at her. 'I'm sorry, Bradfield, honestly. You must think I do it on purpose.'

'Don't you?' Laura asked icily, realising that it had

happened yet again. Now she wondered if Jon really wanted her with him in Devon or if he had merely been dutifully polite in asking her along.

'I hope you don't mind, Laura, if I circulate a bit,' Jon said lightly, as she tied his bow tie for him. She was expert, she had told him, having often done the same for her father. 'We are expected to at these dos.'

'Of course you must circulate,' she insisted. 'Fancy having to explain that to me! You forget I was on the sidelines for years myself, waiting for the great consultants to ask me to dance or join them in a drink.'

She smiled up at him.

'Go on!' he said. 'You were never *waiting* for them, they were falling over themselves to ask you,' and he chucked her under the chin and turned to shrug into the dinner-jacket she was holding out for him. 'How do I look?'

'Absolutely splendid, as always,' she assured him.

'I think you look rather splendid, too,' he said. 'Is that a new dress? I like it.'

She forbore to remind him that it wasn't a new dress and he had admired it previously, which was why she was wearing it on this occasion. She didn't know whether to be flattered or irritated by his observation. Maybe he would say she looked splendid in a flour sack. It was just words—conventional phrases nice people used on each other.

This was the occasion of Thornsea's civic dinner to medical staff, wives, or ladies of their choice. It was held annually, in June, in the Town Hall, and dancing followed. The town's general practitioners were invited, as well as the staffs of both Millerdown and the Cottage. Only a few housemen were on duty at both hospitals, and there was no doubt that some of the guests would be called out before the evening was over. Laura hoped Jon would not be one of them, for he had recently lost a valuable registrar to a senior appointment in London, and had, consequently, been busier than any one man had any right to be.

She was introduced, in the lounge-hall of the Town Hall, to doctors and wives she hadn't yet met, officially, though she had spoken on the phone to most of them, and then they all went in to dinner. She saw Eve Trevor was the guest of Dr Falconer and, as usual, bubbling over with brittle *joie de vivre*. Eve was in black, and looked very beautiful indeed. Laura again wondered why Jon hadn't been able to see anything in her.

By the time the dancing commenced in the adjoining Elizabethan ballroom, she wondered anew, in a different vein, for after dancing the opening waltz with his wife, Jon had squeezed her arm and gone off in Sister Trevor's direction like a pin to a magnet. The foxtrot they danced had been encored, and at the end of it only Jon and Eve were on the floor, obviously moving like a single unit in a perfection they could not have achieved without some practice.

'Hospital champions three years ago,' came a voice in her decidedly jealous ear. 'We held a sort of "Come Dancing", and those two won the sherry. It was drunk at a party, afterwards, in Eve's room. She wasn't married in those days. I was invited, but my firm had an emergency and I missed the celebration. In those days I'd have laid fifty to one on those two having a more permanent sort of partnership.'

'Why are you telling me this, Dr Falconer?' Laura looked up to ask.

'Because I thought I detected some green in that eye of yours. But you needn't fret, you know. There's no comparison.'

'Whatever are you talking about, Doctor?' Laura asked, having watched Jon and Eve retire to the bar, laughing, to celebrate their performance on the dance floor, no doubt.

'I'm talking about you and Evie. She looks like a million, doesn't she? She always did. A well-dressed shop-window, is our Evie, only there's no stock-room behind.'

'Dr Falconer!'

'And stop that nonsense, Laura! All this formality between friends.'

'Friends?' she almost squeaked. She had seen him twice since the episode in the office which had so upset Jon. He had called once to see one of his patients on her ward, and on another occasion he had met her in the park, with Simon. They had chatted for half an hour, mostly about the baby.

'Yes, friends. I'm a friendly chap. But you're trying so hard to dislike me, because his nibs does, that it just isn't real. I won't be disliked by proxy, so there!'

Laura remembered how she had once insisted, when she was being persecuted by her colleagues, that nobody could choose either her friends or her enemies for her. Miles Falconer had done her no harm, so far as she was aware.

'Of course I don't dislike you, Dr Falconer,' she said quite gaily. 'I scarcely know you.'

'That can be remedied,' he said quickly. 'May I have the pleasure?'

Laura had seen, beyond him, Jon ordering Eve Trevor's glass to be recharged with whatever she was drinking. 'Thank you,' she said, feeling unaccountably like a ship adrift, and together they performed quite a creditable quickstep.

'I'll be back,' said Miles Falconer, as he relinquished her at the end of the dance, 'when I've done my duty by one or two of my colleagues' wives, and this time I'd like to buy *you* a drink. O.K.?'

Though Laura hoped and prayed that Jon would come back regularly to dance with her, she was disappointed. She would not stand looking like a wallflower, so she danced with Dr Groves, and then with Mr Richmond, the gynaecologist, who remarked that he hoped she liked his cottage in Devon. 'Tell me if there's anything lacking,' he urged. 'Since I lost my wife I miss a woman's viewpoint of holiday necessities. Things like pillow-cases and spoons.'

'I was sorry to hear about Mrs Richmond,' Laura said quickly.

'Yes, I miss her. But she suffered—I wouldn't want her back like that.'

After this Laura missed Jon, *and* Eve Trevor. She quickly surrendered to Miles Falconer's arms before she could put two and two together to make five. She felt a little harder and brighter after the waltz and a gin and bitter lemon at the bar.

'You're a very beautiful woman,' Miles told her huskily, 'with the mystery of a deep lake. What is in you, Laura? What depths are still untapped?'

'How very poetical you are, Miles! A deep lake—*me*? How absurd!'

'Yes, a deep, deep lake. All still on top, but a man feels nervous that he could drown in you.'

Laura drank in the flattery with the gin. Maybe she was thirsty for it and that the words came from the lips of the wrong man didn't count for very much at that moment. It was pleasant to be told such things, to be made to feel important to somebody.

Her head was on Miles Falconer's shoulder as the lights were dimmed for the last waltz, and her eyes were closed. She opened them as though an ophthalmoscope had flashed upon her and there was Jon's bright blue gaze staring and Eve Trevor in his arms. She clung the more, sagged the more, and was more unhappy than she had imagined possible.

'Had a good time?' Jon asked in the car.

'Marvellous. And you?'

'Not bad. I could see you were quite popular, so I left you to it while I went off with Eve.'

'You went off with Eve?' she asked politely.

'I tried to tell you, but you were in a huddle with Falconer. Somebody had to go and put a fractured femur on traction for the night, and Eve offered to be my chauffeuse. I thought you hadn't missed me,' he said jovially.

'No,' she agreed, 'I didn't,' wondering why she was lying. 'I enjoyed your dancing exhibition earlier,' she lied again.

'Oh that!' he was smiling in the darkness. 'I didn't even think I could dance at one time, but you find you can do some things with some people. In days past, when the world was young, Eve and I discovered our foxtrot was quite something. She wondered if we'd remembered, and we had. Funnily enough, we fell over each other's feet in the waltz.'

'Still, you tried,' Laura said, apparently ingenuously.

'Whereas your waltz, with Falconer, was quite perfect. One could say you were moulded together.'

'Oh, then you noticed?' Laura asked.

'Who couldn't?' Jon demanded, and somehow she knew he was no longer smiling and that tit for tat was not a pleasant game to play.

They were both tired, but that was not the reason they didn't make love that night.

Several things happened all together in June and one of them was a heat wave, which bleached the lawns of the large houses surrounding Thornsea as a ban went out on all garden watering and general wastage. Laura had three patients in plaster jackets, and they suffered in the heat from irritations of the skin and unreachable tickles. Though most institutions are concerned to keep their premises suitably heated in winter, they are usually surprised at the constancy of the sun, in a tolerable summer, and fail to keep out the heat. Most patients groaned even under a sheet, and there were many hundredweights of ice-cream consumed for dessert instead of the more usual milk puddings and steamed jam roll. Nurses became fractious with one another as they passed each other in full sail, hot, sweaty and hustled as they were to get through their unrelenting routines. Laura left the hectic life of the ward for a decidedly more hectic life at home, for, at nineteen months, when Laura had despaired of her stepson ever deciding to move in an upright position, Simon not only walked but seemed to charge around the house in a state of chuckling delight at his discovery. He was a strong baby, and had moved around for months, most athletically, on his plump behind. He had worn out dozens of pairs of overalls during this time. Now his new overalls still were spankingly smart, but his baby slippers suffered instead. He had to have sturdy sandals, and obviously, in the June heat, had much more energy than the adults around him. Cathy was worn out on this particular day, and Laura told her to go and lie down and take the rest of the day off.

Trying to keep Simon in one room was impossible. He had mastered the art of turning knobs and was anxious to explore. He was bored with the garden, where he had spent the morning, and kept Laura busy trotting after him to see that he did no damage. As they went through the hall, Laura noticed a message scribbled on the telephone pad in Cathy's writing.

'Dr Warwick——' (she always referred to him as Doctor) '—Sister Trevor wants you to meet her for lunch. She says you know the place.'

Laura's blood ran cold. It was a month since the Town Hall dance and she had never quite recovered from that. What *was* going on between Jon and Eve Trevor? Did the fact of her being a married woman make her more attractive now that he was a married man?

Crash! came from behind and there was Simon, his mouth in an 'O' of shock and surprise and Jon's favourite Wedgwood vase in smithereens all around him.

'Oh, Simon, naughty!' she scolded, and he immediately began to cry in a helpless, sobbing baby way. 'Never mind,' she then comforted. 'You're tired, you rascal, and you won't admit it. Mummy will give you a wash and put you in the pushchair and we'll go to to the park, where you can run about on the grass. Simon want to go to the park?'

'Park,' he said, with a final hiccoughing sob.

'And we'll take a ball, shall we?'

She tried to collect her thoughts as she washed the baby and put him in a cool cotton romper-suit. The telephone message had shocked her, she didn't realise that Jon and Eve Trevor met at any but public functions. She also had a shocking private thought that she might be pregnant. Of course she had taken all precautions, after their common decision to put off having a family until Simon was older, but there could have been moments of forgetfulness, especially at times when she was upset, and there had never been a pause in her physical functions before in all her life. Of course it was early days to be sure, but there was a seed of disquieting doubt in her, and it wasn't a thing she fancied announcing to Jon if he was belatedly attracted to another woman.

She thrust the thought from her in the hope that if she failed to acknowledge it it would go away, and changed into a sleeveless dress of golden yellow, which made her look marvellous, like a daffodil, though she had no eyes for her appearance at that moment.

Simon slept in the pushchair on the way to the park, but she already knew that he could recharge his energy in only ten minutes and then keep going for hours. She sat down on the grass of the park, under an elm-tree, and waited for the sleeping babe to demand to be free of the restraining harness. It was so hot and so still and she wished it would rain, even though they would both get wet. Only one white cloud floated like a gauze scarf overhead, and it contained not rain but thistledown. She watched it until her eyes became leaden and she slipped into a heavy, dream-laden sleep.

She was having a terrible, violent quarrel with Jon which she couldn't bear. 'Why are you spying on me?' he demanded harshly, with those flashing blue eyes of his. 'Why are you always in my way?'

'In your way, Jon?' she echoed. 'You have to love me, it's your duty. Love me! Love me!'

'Love *you*?' he gave an awful laugh which shrilled into

a cackle and then he had changed into a monster and she tried to scream, awoke and saw the sky, clear and blue as his eyes and there was nobody near her, only an empty pushchair.

An *empty* pushchair?

Remembrance returned sharply and she looked about her, called 'Simon! Simon!' quite sharply. She looked at her wrist-watch. She had only slept for about eleven minutes, and he might not have wakened immediately. She looked at the harness on the pushchair and the straps had been undone. Could Simon . . .? No, he never had . . . he couldn't . . . the alternative was too awful, and she dashed into the shrubbery behind her. He just *had* to be there, somewhere. But he wasn't. Perhaps owing to the heat there weren't many people in the park, only one young mother with a toddler on the other side and an elderly couple on a bench in the shade. Dragging the empty pushchair, Laura crossed an interminable expanse of grass and asked the young mother, 'Excuse me, but have you seen my little boy anywhere?'

'How old?' asked the girl—she only looked about nineteen. 'My Timmy's two,' she added proudly.

'Simon's not yet two,' Laura said distractedly. 'Please think! I was over there, and I closed my eyes. When I woke up——'

'But I've only just come, haven't I?' the other said rather sharply. 'I didn't even see you. I was that glad to get off my feet, I can tell you. The shops are killing in this weather.'

The elderly couple were alarmed for her, but couldn't help, either. Laura went back across the park and looked in the shrubbery a second time, but again without success. There were railings all round the park, and even a baby couldn't squeeze through them, but there were four ways in, and all wide open. There was a limited amount of traffic on the roads. When Laura found a bright orange ball she recognised in the gutter, she really panicked. She asked a woman coming from the town if she had seen a baby running about.

'A baby, *alone?*' The woman looked almost offended. 'After that case in the High Street a couple of months back, where a baby was taken off by one of these unbalanced people? You ought to be more careful, now shouldn't you?'

Now Laura had all the horrors presented to her, and in the police station she was almost incoherent.

'Now, now, we'll find him,' soothed the burly desk sergeant. 'Anybody could have picked him up and be giving him an ice-lolly at this very moment. It's hardly likely anybody would have ignored a little chap like that running loose, now is it? Bare feet, I believe you said?'

'I was going to let him play on the grass,' Laura whimpered. 'I didn't mean to fall asleep.'

'I know, I know. Feel like nodding off myself, in this weather. I'll send for a pot of tea. I'm sure we could both do with one.'

Half an hour later the force of local law was searching for the missing child and Laura had asked permission to inform Jon herself. When she got through to Millerdown he had just finished operating and sounded rather sharp.

'Well, Laura? I'm wanting to get under a shower. It was rather warm under those lamps on a day like this.'

'I know, Jon. Something awful happened. I—I don't know how to tell you.'

'Tell me, for God's sake!' he urged. 'Is the kid sick?'

'He—he's missing. I—I lost him in the park.'

'You—lost—him—in—the—park?' he repeated, slowly and incredulously. 'How could any fool—I mean—anybody do that?'

'I fell asleep. When I woke up he'd gone.'

'What do you mean—gone?'

'The straps of the harness in the pushchair were undone and he wasn't there. I looked everywhere, dashed about, asking everybody in sight. No one had seen anything.'

Jon's voice had risen a tone. 'That harness buckle was

baby-proof,' he said flatly. 'It cost a lot because it had to
be so. Unless the kid's a genius he couldn't have undone
it himself. Therefore one must presume somebody else
undid it and—and took him. Have you informed the
police?'

'Yes. I'm at the police station now. They're all out
with walkie-talkies, dogs and—and everything. I've been
told to go home and wait there.'

She realised she was speaking into a dead instrument.
Jon wasn't there any more. Like she had been, he must
now be feeling frantic with anxiety.

'Could you please get me a taxi?' she asked the kindly
desk sergeant. 'I don't think I could walk home.'

'There's a Panda car going your way now, Mrs Warwick. They'll drop you off. Try not to worry too much.'

But of course she worried. Cathy had got up and began
to cry when she heard the news. Jon arrived home looking grey, still in the green cotton suit in which, covered
by a gown, he had recently operated. It seemed eternity,
with nobody saying anything, before the telephone rang
and Jon lifted the receiver. He said hardly anything, only
'yes' and 'I see', but Laura imagined a little colour had
crept back into his face.

'That was the police,' he said in a tight voice. 'They've
found the blighter.'

Laura gave a little yelp and sat down. If a chair hadn't
been near she would simply have collapsed where she
stood. 'He's O.K.,' Jon went on in that stranger's voice.
'He'll be here any moment and all will be made clear.'

Cathy watched the drive like a hawk and announced
the fact when a strange car drew up out of which stepped
a young policeman and a man carrying Simon.

'He's all tuckered out, bless him!' Cathy flung open the
door to take the sleeping baby from—Laura stared—
Miles Falconer.

The policeman asked, 'Can you identify this gentleman, Mrs Warwick?'

'Ye—es,' Laura found her voice trembled with a peculiar vocal palsy. 'This is Dr Falconer, a partner of Dr Murchison's.'

'Right, that's what he said. I just wanted your confirmation. I'll leave Dr Falconer to explain what happened and get back to my partner.'

'Thank you, Constable,' Jon remembered to say, and then three pairs of eyes were on Dr Falconer.

'I'm sorry! I'm sorry!' he said quickly. 'It was a joke which went a bit wrong, that's all. It could have happened to anybody.'

'What did happen, exactly?' Jon asked starkly.

'Well, I saw Laura asleep on the grass in the park, and the little chap was wriggling to get out of the chair. So I let him out and played with him for a tick, but all he wanted to do was run off. I thought I'd better strap him back in, or wake Laura up, when I decided I'd teach her a lesson. Well, I could have been anybody, a kidnapper, or worse. The kid had dashed off while I was trying to make up my mind, and as I picked him up I thought I'd pop him in the car and run him once or twice round the park, keeping an eye on Laura's reactions when she saw he'd gone. I really didn't mean to cause any fuss. But I hadn't allowed for the traffic-lights at Park Avenue and Deane Street, where an articulated lorry had jack-knifed across the road. All the traffic was diverted down Queen's Drive, and when I got back to the park I couldn't see you, Laura, or the pushchair. I cruised around looking for you, but had no luck, and was just about to phone you at home when a bobby wanted to know whose the kid was. I had to go to the police station then, and tell my story, and a nice fool I felt telling it, I can assure you. The rest youu know, but I've never been made to feel like a criminal in all my life before.'

As he started to explain, it seemed to Laura that the core of a volcano stirred within her. This erupted with greater degrees of violence until, as he finished speaking, she hurled herself on Miles Falconer like a mad thing, beating at him unmercifully with tightly-balled fists. It was Jon who hauled her off, still beating at the air, and Jon who told Dr Falconer to leave.

'I've said I'm sorry,' Miles said aggrievedly. 'It could have happened to anybody.'

'It could only have happened to a mindless moron,' Jon said sharply. 'Now get out before I throw you out!'

Cathy was staring at Laura, who was still making lunging motions with her hands.

'She's upset,' he explained to the girl. 'Will you take Simon and bath him and put him to bed? I know it's still early, but he's had quite a day.'

He lifted Laura up as though she was a doll and followed Cathy up the stairs. Once in the bedroom he dropped her quite roughly on to the bed.

'You must be very angry, Jon,' she whimpered.

'I am pretty livid,' he agreed.

'What are you doing?' He was busy in the bathroom.

Without answering he shoved a glass of white liquid at her.

'Here, drink this.'

'What is it?'

'You know very well what it is. It's to knock you out for an hour or two.'

'I don't think I want to be knocked out.'

'*Drink it!*' he said in a voice of doom, and she obeyed without more ado.

'Now before you leave the world,' he said in a quieter, but no less menacing, tone of voice, 'I don't want to see your friend Falconer in this house again. I don't want him to touch *my son*. What he does with you is your own business, but not here. Understand? Not here.'

'What do you mean what he does with me, Jon? Gosh, but you have given me something strong!'

'I mean that we live in a goldfish bowl, you and I, and he's inclined to boast of his conquests.'

'Conquesh?' she demanded petulantly. 'What conquesh? What about you and her, eh? Do you boash of your conquesh?'

'You're inarticulate, Laura,' he said scathingly. 'Give in and go to sleep. I have to get back to my job. I seem to think I left a few ends untied.'

'I hate *you*!' she managed to fling after him before she had to surrender to the smothering of consciousness demanded by the drug he had given her.

For two days Miss Trueblood had to find temporary help for her orthopaedic wards. Sister Bradfield was reported to be unwell, but of course Matron knew all about the scare over the baby. Most of the hospital did by now. Eve Trevor had heard it from the horse's mouth of Miles Falconer and saw only the funny side of it.

'I believe Jon wanted to kill him,' she told her cronies. 'Well, you know those two never did like each other, and then for Miles to do a fool thing like that. What with pinching his kid and wanting to seduce his wife, you'd think that was asking for trouble, wouldn't you?'

'You do say some terrible things, Trevor,' Mahmoud protested. 'How do you know there's anything between Mr Warwick's wife and Dr Falconer?'

'Well, I don't for sure.' Trevor looked knowing, however. 'You weren't at the Town Hall hop, were you? Well, you should just have seen them swooning all over one another in the last waltz. I mean if you don't want to start gossip why behave like that in public, eh? Miles told me straight out that he fancies her. He's made up his mind that she's not happy with Jon. I don't think Jon's happy with her, and that just anything might happen before long.'

'I bet you don't half hope so!' said Martyn, sharply for her, 'I don't think you ever got over the fact somebody could get along without you, when you'd made an obvious offer.'

'Vicious old spinster!' was Sister Trevor's retort to this. Her back gave a twinge shortly after this, but she knew if she mentioned the fact that nobody was in the mood to offer her sympathy.

'If we'd been a normal married couple,' Laura said clearly, 'we'd have had a flaming row and thrown things. As it is——' and she shrugged.

'You have the idea that in all normal marriages there is shrieking and violence?' Jon was smiling but without humour. 'What a funny lot of married friends you must have.'

'I know what we have isn't normal,' Laura insisted. 'I thought it wasn't too bad at first, but now there's too much of getting on the other's nerves. I can't do my job properly any more. Before my patients suffer I think I ought to hand in my notice.'

'I am sorry you are so disillusioned by our venture, Laura. I really am. What can I say? What can I do?'

'It's nobody's fault, Jon. Don't blame yourself. Falling in love with someone is obviously the best foundation for marriage, still. But where there's no love something has to take its place. I feel we're in danger of actively disliking each other before long. I couldn't bear that.'

'I'm sorry you feel this way, Laura.'

'If it had been a love match would you have been suspicious of me and Miles Falconer? Of course not. And I wouldn't keep coupling you and Sister Trevor, knowing that you loved me. So—so there it is,' she finished lamely. 'I think we ought to part, Jon. We came together for Simon's sake, but as we are we're no good to him, or each other.'

'I wouldn't hold you in unhappy thrall for the world, Laura. Maybe I'm keeping you from someone with whom you could be happy. What do you suggest?'

'I've been giving the matter a lot of thought. Jane's baby is due next month. I could make that my excuse and join my people in Australia.'

'What would you tell them?'

'Nothing, at first. Gradually I suppose they'd gather that things hadn't worked out. They wouldn't demand to know. They're not like that.'

'I would have liked to have met them. I really mean that. Your mother has taken me to her heart by correspondence. I shall miss her letters.'

'Yes,' now Laura's smile was like a wound in her lovely face, 'we do seem to get on so well with everybody but each other. Well, at least we've learned what not to do.'

'You don't think we should have another stab at things? Consciously trying . . .?'

'Oh, Jon! With me afraid to say "You're late again", and you telling me the burnt stew is *Cordon bleu*? That's not marriage. Simon's too bright not to spot the phoneyness of it all very quickly.'

'Well—' he shrugged helplessly—'I must leave you free to act as you wish, Laura. I can see you're determined to end things. Would it help if I moved out of here for the month of your notice? I could say I'm doing a refresher course, have to be free to doo some quiet reading.'

'Would you, Jon?'

'Certainly. I'll pack a bag and just go. Then I'll take my leave and go to Bideford, as arranged. I don't suppose you——?'

'No, I shouldn't think so. You'll have Cathy and maybe a housekeeper, living in, would be the correct solution for you, after all, when you return. In no time at all I'll be forgotten, but in any case I don't think there's much that isn't either known, or suspected, about our arrangement. As you said on the day Simon was missing, we do live in a goldfish bowl.'

Within the hour he was gone, and she was sighing with a kind of agonising relief that she could let down her guard, at last. She found it easy to confide in Cathy that the "Doctor" was staying away for a few weeks, to do some studying.

'It's quite impossible to concentrate with a lively baby in the house,' she explained.

'Fancy that! Is Doctor still learning, then?'

'One has to keep up with all the latest trends, Cathy. There are always developments in medical matters.'

She hadn't told Jon that she had already handed in her notice to Matron. Torn in half as she now was, confused, mentally battered and not yet recovered from the awful guilt of feeling she might have been responsible for harm befalling the baby, she had felt it was all too likely that she could suffer a lapse such as had overtaken her in the past, and with such a loss of confidence she was better removed from the hospital scene. Miss Trueblood had asked if she considered Staff Nurse Pringle was up to promotion, and Laura couldn't think of anyone more deserving of such an honour and responsibility. So she had three weeks yet to serve, and beyond that she couldn't either think or plan. She could go home—she knew where the keys were—or she could take a little holiday and allow time to heal where it would. She knew she wouldn't really fly out to Australia. Jane's joy in the birth of her child must not be shadowed by the other sister's unhappiness, and that she was unhappy in the failure of her marriage was only too true. Worse than leaving Jon was living with him and watching him grow to hate her. He had hated her when Simon disappeared; she had never seen him so unapproachable. Also he obviously didn't know her, or he could not have imagined she would ever cheapen herself or dishonour her marriage. Parting would cause much inconvenience, but better inconvenience than downright unhappiness.

Gradually Laura dropped hints to Cathy about several matters.

'I may not be coming with you to Bideford, Cathy. I— I have a sick relative . . .' white lies, little white lies . . . 'I may have to go to her,' and when the girl had made a few sympathetic noises, 'I think the doctor would agree to your taking a friend on holiday. Would you like that? He'll be fishing and so on. A friend would be company for you.'

What would he tell Cathy when she didn't come back? Well, that was his problem. Would he ask for a divorce, eventually? After all, she was deserting him.

Somehow she faced her last week's work at the Cottage Hospital without feeling nearer solutions to anything. She would go home for a few days; that she had decided. Beyond that she was a traveller with a wide, featureless desert ahead of her.

'Here we are again!' greeted Eve Trevor, holding a small suitcase.

'I—I don't understand,' Laura said woodenly.

'I'm your patient again. Just for one night. I'm having a spinal manipulation to try to clear up my trouble once and for all. There isn't a staff bed at Millerdown, so Jon said he'd do me here.'

'I wasn't told.'

'No. Well, I am a rush job. I want to go off on leave on Saturday. No doubt there's information about me on your desk at this very moment, but I have starved myself, take my word for that, and I'm to have a G.A. and manipulation at three this afternoon. Tell me where I'm living and I'll pop into bed.'

All this was confirmed as Laura sat down at her desk and saw a clip-board with Sister Trevor's notes affixed to it and an explanatory note from Jon attached.

'Dear Sister——' how formal! and yet he had to be formal in the circumstances. 'Sister Trevor still complains of spasmodic pain in sacral and lumbar regions of spine. No sign of slipped discs. Pain may be due to muscular rigidity. Propose performing full spinal manipulation, under general anaesthetic, at fifteen hundred hours today, July the fourteenth. Premedication as follows. . . .'

When she accompanied Sister Trevor to the theatre she would see Jon, as she saw him some part of every day. They were extremely polite and businesslike, always, at such times. It was difficult to imagine that she had once warmed his frozen body with her own. In fact it was better not to imagine, or remember.

So she eventually delivered her patient, and saw Jon, and heard him addressing her in a more personal tone.

'Time must be getting on for you,' he observed.

'Yes. Not much longer now.'

'I'm not asking what you're doing. It's none of my business. I mean you'd tell me, I hope, if there was anything I could do?'

'Yes, of course. I'll be leaving The Arbor tomorrow.'

'So soon?' he looked startled. 'Well, I suppose I'll have to know where I can reach you—if ever . . .?'

'I'll tell my lawyer to get in touch with yours. I won't be taking all my things initially. I'll have to send for them.'

'Of course. Well——' he hesitated and held out his hand. 'Good luck Laura! I mean that.'

'You too, Jon.' She didn't know how she found her way back to the ward for the dimming of her eyes. She wanted to cry her heart out in the privacy of her office, but outside was a visitor. 'Mrs Kershaw!' Laura exclaimed.

The elderly woman was on elbow crutches and her hands were still gnarled, but she got along quite competently on her feet in sensible orthopaedic shoes. A younger woman said gladly, 'Mum wanted to come and say a proper thank you, Sister. She say's it's all thanks to you. We're taking her back to live with us in Toronto.'

'You must be the daughter,' Laura shook hands, looking from one to the other. 'I remember reading the letter which told of your proposed visit, and how we all rushed to get your mother upright in time.'

'Which you did, bless you!' Mrs Kershaw beamed.

'Will you come in for a cuppa?'

'Well——' the daughter hesitated.

'Too much to do,' Mrs Kershaw laughed. 'These Canadians don't half hustle. Anyway, you're always pushed for time yourself, Sister. No doubt somebody else needs you more'n I do, now. So we'll say goodbye.'

'It's been lovely seeing you looking so fit,' Laura watched her ex-patient walk away on her crutches, turn to wave and then follow her daughter into the lift. 'That's the ending of a good chapter in my life,' she decided.

163

CHAPTER NINE

LAURA was working a full day on her last at Thornsea Cottage Hospital. It was Staff Nurse Pringle's day off duty, and Sister Groves, who usually took over in the afternoon, was suffering from a gastro-enteric infection. After a two-hour lunch break Laura anticipated being on duty until eight p.m. She had informed Cathy of this fact.

At six o'clock Eve Trevor was groaning her way out of the anaesthetic. Laura was quietly confiscating cigarettes and matches from the bedside locker. There was a day-room where patients were allowed to smoke, but never in their beds.

'God, he's broken my back, I'm sure,' the patient complained. 'The damned cure's worse than the disease. Hey!' she said sharply. 'Where're my fags?'

'You'll get them back tomorrow, when you leave,' Laura said.

'You don't have to dot all the i's with a colleague, do you? I wanna fag.'

'Sorry!' Laura said firmly. 'Go to sleep, Sister.'

'But I'm in pain.'

'Hang on for an hour and I'll give you something for the night.'

Ron Trevor came in a little later and left, saying, 'We were talking and Eve just went to sleep. Do her more good than my yakking, I expect.'

When Laura looked in the side-ward Sister Trevor was still sleeping, so she went to the office and wrote up the notes for Night Sister. Fancy, her last night in this place where she had suffered every kind of mauling and yet been happier than ever before in her life. What a fateful place Thornsea had been for her! And even now it hadn't finished with her.

She smelled burning before she had finished writing. As she jumped up she could see smoke creeping along the corridor outside, and it was coming from the side-ward where Sister Trevor lay. Laura put her finger on the red fire-button before opening the door and seeing her patient lying apparently unconscious, in the middle of smouldering bedclothes. With the inrush of air some of the smoke broke into the brilliance of flames.

Only Nurse Rodriguez was on duty at that hour, along with Laura, and only she witnessed the usually immaculate ward Sister emerge from a blazing room dragging a patient after her.

'Sister! Your hair is afire!' screamed the girl.

'Can you shut that door, Nurse?' Laura asked calmly. 'That will confine the blaze.'

Now there was help at hand—porters with extinguishers and Dr Dawson, who had been attending a patient in a nearby ward, and Matron, who naturally wanted to know exactly what had happened.

Poor stupid Trevor had nearly caused her own death by her addiction to tobacco and her determination never to obey simple hospital rules.

'She got some from her silly husband, obviously,' Matron concluded. 'I want to see that young man as soon as he gets here. Now you, Sister. I'm sorry about your lovely hair. You've lost quite a bit, haven't you? How do you feel?'

'Not too bad. Relieved it was no worse.'

'I think you behaved with remarkable promptitude. That girl owes her life to you. Oh, yes, she does. I'll see everybody knows it, too.'

'I—I'd rather you didn't say much in that vein, Matron.'

'Rubbish! A heroine's a heroine.'

'I'd like to go home, Matron, if you don't mind.'

'I should think you would. I'll get you a taxi. This is your last day with us, isn't it? What a curtain, eh, my dear?'

'I'll call in tomorrow to empty my locker.'

The next day she said goodbye, as though temporarily, to Cathy, and kissed Simon. 'You'll watch him, won't you, Cathy?'

'Oh, yes, Mrs Warwick. Don't you worry about the little rascal.'

At the hospital was ex-Nurse Pringle, unfamiliar in navy-blue.

'I believe you recommended me, Sister? Thanks a lot.'

'You recommended yourself, my dear.'

'I get my belt at lunch-time. Do you remember when you——?'

'I'll say I do!' Laura smiled. 'I hope it'll be a happier occasion for you.'

'Er—Sister Trevor wanted to see you.'

'Well, I didn't want to stay long. I have a lot to do.'

'She made me promise I'd send you in. She's in number four. She is a bit shocked, poor dear, on top of the soreness.'

'Very well.' Laura went along to the small room which was usually kept for emergencies. Down the corridor the workmen were ripping out scorched floorboards in the damaged wide-ward. An acrid smell of burning still pervaded the atmosphere.

'Sister——?' Eve Trevor looked very pale against the white pillow. She began to cry bitterly. 'Here, what's this?' Laura asked gently. 'I must go if I upset you.'

'No, don't go. P—please don't go. I—I might have died if it hadn't been for you.'

'Now don't be silly. I happened to be there. If it hadn't been me it would have been somebody else.'

'But it *was* you, and anybody had to be damned brave to do what you did. You could have left me and shouted for help—that's what I'd have done—but you were on fire. Cool as a cucumber and on fire. They told me.'

'They're exaggerating. I only lost a hank of hair.'

'What about your hand, then? And the blister on your neck?'

166

'I'll live,' Laura shrugged.

'So will I, thanks to you, but some things I find I can't live with. I have to clear the air.'

'Oh, dear, Sister! Look, I'm not your confessor. Just get fit and go off on your leave. I really have to go——'

'You're leaving Jon, aren't you?'

Laura looked startled for a moment, off guard.

'What makes you say a thing like that?'

'Because he's terribly uneasy when you're mentioned. He called in to see me first thing this morning. He didn't even know about you—what you did. He said some rubbish about a course he was taking; that he hadn't been home for some time.'

'Actually that's true,' Laura said thinly. 'You mustn't concern yourself about other people, Sister. Just get better.'

'Look! I *have* to say things which may shock you. I have been against you from the first. I don't really understand myself in this regard. I admit I used to think Jon Warwick was mine for snapping my fingers. Well, he wasn't and this fact took all my self-confidence away. I suppose I was the typical woman scorned, and reacted with suitable hellish fury. I felt I could never forgive him. I hated Jean when she married him, and him through her when things went wrong. If I'd hoped he would turn to me when Jean went off him, I had another think coming, and he had merely added more fuel to the fires of destruction in me. When you came along and sort of stuck up for him, and then actually married him, I wanted you both to burn in Hades. I couldn't do anything bad enough. I couldn't achieve my ends through being nasty all the time, so I tried to do it by being nice, and had more success. I made Miles Falconer my accessory, and at first he played up. Then he really did fall for you, and I let Jon know this in the sweetest way possible, because that's the way one uncomplainingly takes a bitter dose, wrapped up in sugar. I let you think, when I could, that Jon was rather keen on me. I even telephoned messages

167

to your house which must have been double-dutch to him, hoping you'd see them and think the worst. And I gleaned my harvest through pretending friendship for you, through your cleaning woman, Mrs Gee. Her sister keeps a little shop near where I live. I buy my cigarettes there. Your Mrs Gee isn't disloyal, but she *is* a gossip. I've played you off against each other until I can tell, the way you both react, that my tactics are working. That busines with Miles and the baby really hit Jon where it hurt, because Jean used to taunt him with the fact that Miles could possibly be Simon's father.'

'Youu knew about that?' was torn from Laura.

'Yes, and I know it isn't true. Jean was pretty but terribly undersexed, like some women are. She admitted to me she was terrified of marrying Jon, because he was bound to want all that beastly nonsense. That's the way she spoke about marital relations, like an underdeveloped school kid. She told me when she suspected she was pregnant, and was horrified when it was proved that she was. Jon was responsible, all right, but she didn't give him much joy of it. Even I was ashamed of the way she spoke to him in the hospital, though I was glad at the same time that he was being punished. He should have married normally-sexed old me, was what I privately thought, and it served him right.

'Well, I think the rest you know, but I want to assure you that your husband hasn't a thought in his head for any woman but you. When I befriended him again I had to be bored by hearing how wonderful you were, and how it was second time lucky, and all that nonsense. He hasn't said it for some time, but he goes all blue-eyed and tight-lipped when you're mentioned. That's the way he withdraws when he's hurt. After all, I've had an unrequited love affair with him for some years, and one does learn to read the signs. No, let me finish! Now, I know you've resigned from Thornsea Cottage, and I also know you're supposed to be visiting a sick relative and will not be occupying that Devon cottage. If I read all these things correctly they're the preliminaries to a separation, maybe a divorce, and I should be feeling pretty satisfied with myself. Well, I'm married to Ron Trevor, and I married him for all the wrong reasons, but he's been so good to me that I'm beginning to appreciate my Ron. I want to make him happy, have kids, but I feel I can't find happiness while I'm sort of responsible for somebody else's suffering. So will you make it up with Jon now?'

Laura was pale and felt rather sick. She had felt sick on and off for a day or two, but she couldn't blame her colleague for that.

'Sister Trevor,' she said huskily, 'you're now as convincing in your role of conciliator as you were in that of persecutor a short while ago. How does one know when you're sincere?'

'Oh, I am! I am!'

'Well, even if you are, what difference can it make if damage is already done? If you'd been responsible for a train smash, you could say you were sorry, but it wouldn't wipe out the fatalities, would it? You'd still see the wreckage all around. Well, you may have done a mischief you'll never be able to see, and nobody can mend.'

'Can't you try, for my sake, if not for your own? You do love Jon, don't you?'

'I think you're the last person with whom I could ever discuss my innermost feelings, Sister Trevor. I'm sorry, but I can't confide what I feel to anybody.'

'Well, Jon loves you. When he was here this morning he was frantic to see you, to make sure you were O.K. He was about to dash off home when somebody phoned him from Millerdown. I heard him say 'Damn!' and then he looked in on me again. He said when I was better he'd wring my neck on several counts, then he dashed off. You see I'd already told him how I'd tried to make trouble, the same things I've told you.'

'Only you told him how I'd confessed to you that he was my absolute dream man, I suppose?'

Eve Trevor actually looked nonplussed.

'Look, it hasn't been easy making myself out to be a heel. I know how Jon feels because I know *him*; you I don't know very well, because we got off on the wrong foot from the start, I suppose. I don't know how you feel about him, only that you seemed happier at one time than you do now. I've come clean and I don't know what else I can do. If it *was* a train-smash I suppose I could hire a crane and clear away the debris, at least. That, humbly, is what I want to do now.'

'Well, thanks,' Laura couldn't actually smile, she grimaced instead. 'I don't quite know how to put this, but if you did do any damage to our marriage then it just wasn't good enough. Do you understand? If a third person can undermine what you have, then to my way of thinking it isn't worth having. You may have nothing to blame yourself for.'

'I think you expressed that jolly well, actually,' said Eve. 'What you're saying is you may have been heading for the rocks without my help, or Dr Falconer's. But outsiders can shake the boat. You should meet my mother-in-law some time. If you're going through a bad patch they can make it seem unbearable. At least see Jon when he comes back here. Too many women have hurt that man.'

'He's coming back here?' Laura asked, paling.

'Yes. As soon as he can make it. I was rather hoping he'd walk in.'

'Well, I *don't*,' Laura said flatly. 'I may be unreasonable, but I don't want any reunions with my husband in this room and under your scrutiny. Jon and I don't need any intermediaries. I'll say goodbye, Sister Trevor.'

'Goodbye! At least I tried——'

Laura managed to slip away from her ex-wards undetected. She picked up her suitcase from the porter's cubbyhole and collected her documents from the office.

'There'll be your pay-cheque arriving, Sister,' said the clerk. 'Where shall I send it? I believe you're going on leave?'

'Yes. Would you send any mail and my cheque to my parents' home in Oxfordshire? You have the address there.'

'Certainly, Mrs Warwick.'

She crouched behind the shrubbery as she recognised Jon's car following an ambulance up the drive. Her emotions were chaotic. She had to calm down, find peace and serenity, sit and think, and maybe even just sit. Reaction from the previous evening's events was now setting in and she felt as nervous as a kitten. Jon had the power to break her, that moment, and even though he didn't use it she felt she dared not see him face to face in case there was a kind of final discompositon.

Of course Eve Trevor's revelations had shaken her. That she had even had access to news from The Arbor via Mrs Gee! It seemed nothing that had occurred was secret or sacred.

She caught the train to Cambridge, and changed there. At three o'clock she was opening up the house in Cobwick where she decided to stay until some healing process took place. She was mentally, morally, even physically bruised by events. The blister on her neck throbbed. It might be turning septic, she thought, without being unduly perturbed. Burns often did turn septic.

She rang old Dr Wales asking for an appointment. He said why not that same evening, at seven, and come to dinner. She refused the dinner invitation but accepted the appointment, saying she needed an early night. She would *have* to know, and the sooner the better.

'Yes, my dear, you're surely pregnant,' said Dr Wales with a satisfied rubbing of hands. 'I always like to tell that to someone I brought into the world. It makes me think they're all members of my own family. Happy?'

'Well, a bit confused, actually,' Laura said tremulously. 'It wasn't intended. I don't suppose I've been very professional about this.'

'Balderdash! You're married, aren't you? Well, what are you fretting about? You and Jane in the same year, eh? Your dad'll be like a dog with two tails. Well, I'll do the final pathological test in the morning, but I think you know as well as I do that you have all the classic signs and symptoms?'

'Yes, I know it's true.'

'Shall I book you for delivery?'

At last Laura had to smile. 'Oh, Dr Wales, I don't know where I'll be when I'm delivered! Not here, I shouldn't think.'

'No. Your husband will want to arrange all that, no doubt. But keep in touch, won't you?'

She felt calmer now that she knew for certain. There was nothing like knowing one was going to have a child for making other less tangible problems sink into the background. Jon assumed less importance and so did Laura herself. The unborn babe was the most important person in the whole world. The doctor had looked at her burns, changed the dressings and given her another shot of penicillin. She felt a little better, more comfortable and clearer-headed. Now she knew she had left Jon not because of anger between them but because she loved him with a hopeless devotion that threatened to break her heart because the knowledge was kept retained with her. It would have done no harm to confide her feelings with Jon; he could only feel flattered. While she kept the secret there was no wonder he had suspected her of squandering her emotions elsewhere, especially when a self-confessed enemy had encouraged such suspicions.

After a light supper—she had brought provisions with her—she settled down at her father's writing desk to pen the most difficult letter of her life.

Jon dear——

Today I deliberately avoided you because I wanted to sort myself out without the emotion with which your presence always seems to surround me. I know our marriage was a sort of arrangement, and emotion didn't come into it. Well, not at first. But I don't think I could live with any man and not have any feeling for him. I couldn't have said 'Cherry ripe' on that first occasion without liking you a lot. I say 'like' because there's no word in English which means to love a little. Maybe I broke all the rules because I was soon loving you a lot, and because I couldn't bring myself to tell you (I'm impossibly reserved at times) I felt terribly hurt on occasions when I fancied you slighted me and even seemed to prefer someone else. In fact to shame the devil—I was miserable with jealousy both of your first wife and any other woman you looked at. I thought you had hasted into a marriage of convenience with me and preferred to repent at leisure with somebody else. I know how blind jealousy makes people, and how unkind. I tried to hurt you back, and I'm sorry, because you couldn't help it if you were holding to the rules of our 'friendly marriage' and I was breaking them by falling in love with you and being horribly jealous. In all the confusion this caused me I was careless, and now I'm pregnant. I came to my old family doctor to find out, because I couldn't discuss such a thing with a stranger, and he has confirmed my suspicions. If I go to term the baby is due in January. A winter's child. I don't know whether I should apologise, because things were complicated enough in our affairs without our becoming parents.

I had to be honest with you, Jon. Too long have I kept certain facts from you. I'll accept your decision regarding all our futures without argument, providing you promise not simply to act out of pity. I think you respect me sufficiently to be quite honest with me, in return.

I await your reply. As you see, I'm at my old home for the time being.   LAURA

She read the letter through and didn't feel any urge to alter one word. She had simply written things she had found she was too inarticulate to say. Funny, how anger made it so easy to say one hated, and yet love didn't urge its own confession!

She stamped the envelope after addressing it and went out to the post box, though she knew it wasn't emptied until twelve-thirty-five next day. She felt more settled now the deed was done and terribly sleepy. Some things she dared not think of; Simon's plump reaching arms drawing her head down for a wet baby kiss was one of these. When she had heated some milk she took the pill Dr Wales had given her, and settled in her old bed to sleep.

CHAPTER TEN

THE house was detached and stood in a lane with about half a dozen others of various vintages, from an old stone cottage to a modern Georgian-style near-mansion. It was a quiet place; the gardens were big. Laura awoke wondering who had Lassie, the labrador. Her parents would never put Lassie in kennels. It would be nice to find the old girl and take her for a walk.

The sound of a mower cutting the grass of the lawn brought her to the bedroom window. A startled face looked up at the agitated curtains and the young man stopped the mower and ran for the gate.

'Just a minute!' Laura called. 'Who are you?'

'Who are *you*, more like,' retorted the other, obviously reassured by hearing a female voice. 'I was told the house were empty. The folk've gone abroad.'

'That's right,' Laura agreed. 'They're myy parents. I'm just visiting to collect some of my things.'

'Oh. Then I'll carry on wi' my mowing. I was told to keep all in order. A bit of a gardener, your dad.'

'That's right. I'll give you a cup of coffee in a few minutes.'

She took a shower and regarded her wet body questioningly. Nothing much to see yet, but the precious seed of a human life was nurturing itself within her. A boy? . . . girl? She couldn't imagine. The baby was only an 'it' at present, until it actually came into the world and cried and revealed its own mysterious personality and by the process of the genes of heredity took on this likeness or that.

She dressed and switched the kettle on in the kitchen, put a pan of milk on the stove and some bread in the toaster. Better to eat and get the sickness over. Fortunately it didn't persist. She made a snack for the gardener and took it out on a tray. The mower was there on the back lawn, but not the young man. He came lumbering up the side of the house and relieved her of the tray.

'I told 'im,' he said in a pleasant country burr, 'I told 'im, I did. "You can't park in the lane", I said. "Too narrer." '

'You told whom?' Laura asked politely.

'The gennelman in the big car. Well, it's all right for a minute, but what when the grocery comes up? I told 'im to put it in the garridge.'

'In our garage?' Laura asked.

'Well, he was comin' 'ere, weren't he? The Chestnuts, he said. An' that's 'ere. Thankye, miss,' and he went off down the garden towards the potting shed.

Laura felt all her nerves shrilling before she looked up and saw the one she both longed and dreaded to see. Jon was crunching the gravel of the drive underfoot, his blue eyes like the lens of a high-speed camera upon her. She thought she cried out, but it seemed all strength oozed out of her in that moment. Jon picked her out of a rose-bed and swept her up.

'I'm all right,' she insisted.

'You look it.'

'Honestly,' she pleaded, and he set her down, still examining her pale face with professional eyes. 'The front door's open,' she told him, and led the way inside.

'Nice village,' Jon commented. 'Fairly unspoilt, still.'

'We do get quite a lot of aircraft going over.'

'Who doesn't, these days?' asked Jon.

He didn't say why he had come and she felt faint again, thinking of that telling letter lying in the nearby post box. If she could write it why couldn't she shout it at him, throw herself in his arms?

'You'll have some breakfast with me?' was all she could manage.

175

'Why not?' he said with a grin. 'It won't be the first time, will it? I've been motoring since four a.m.'

'Oh, Jon!' she said, genuinely concerned. 'You must be worn out.'

'No, not yet. Maybe later. Actually summer mornings are so lovely. I was off in what the poets call a roseate dawn and beat most of the traffic.'

'But how did you know where to come?'

'Would you believe instinct?' he asked, as she put a rack of toast on the table and a pot of coffee. 'Maybe that's bit far-fetched. I looked it up in staff records. Fortunately you were still there.'

'Jon, I—I didn't run away, you know. I simply had to get away for a bit.'

'There's a difference, Laura?' he asked.

'You know there is. When you're on top of a picture, or a problem, you can't see it. You have to step back. That's what I've been doing and now I do see things better.'

He leaned towards her, bitterly playful.

'How do I look close up, Laura? Better at a distance, eh?'

'Oh, Jon, don't!'

'I came to ask you if you want a divorce, Laura. We only have to tell our absurd story and I'm sure they'll snuff us out like a candle. They'll probably recommend us to a psychiatrist at the same time.'

'Jon!' she said warningly, and then the nausea welled in her and she stood up. 'Please excuse me a minute,' she gasped, and scampered upstairs to the privacy of the bathroom. 'Sorry about that,' she apologised as she rejoined him. 'I get indigestion lately.'

'Laura,' he said sternly, as though her bobbing up and down was merely a contrived annoyance, 'it wasn't easy coming here. I don't know when I slept or ate last. *I* have indigestion, maybe an ulcer. I feel rotten.'

'I'm sorry. Can I get you anything?'

'No. Just shut up for a minute. I'm reeking of self-pity

and I'm going to wallow for a moment. Yesterday I heard from others that my wife was the heroine of a fire, that she had burns, and I couldn't damned well catch up with her. You dodged me knowing how I must be feeling.'

'Well, I wasn't really hurt. You must have known that.'

'If the scalpel slipped and I suffered one cut, wouldn't you have been concerned for me? Wouldn't you have wanted to see with your own eyes, even though we both knew it was only a scratch?'

'Yes, of course. But——'

'Go on. I'm waiting to hear why you are allowed the refinement of feelings denied to me.'

'Jon! The fire, my burns, they weren't important as they were related to that special time. I was suffering more severe injuries, or thought I was. The rest was merely an inconvenience.'

'Have I messed things up for you, coming here?'

'No, of course not.'

'Then why the swoon? Was it so shocking seeing me?'

'Jon! It wasn't *that*.' She ran a hand over her brow. If only he'd got my letter first! she thought.

'I can see I *am* upsetting you, Laura. I'd better go.'

'No, don't go. Please don't go.'

'Maybe we can learn from that old song which goes, 'Oh no, John, no, John, no-o, John, no,' and manages to sound like an assent?'

She didn't smile. Only a tremulous sigh escaped her.

'I didn't really come to ask about a divorce,' he admitted, 'but if you must have one then I may be able to persuade Eve Trevor to weekend in gay Paree with me. Just say the word.'

'Actually I think you mmay be too late there,' Laura said flatly. 'She seems to be falling in love with her husband.'

'Ah! She told you that, did she? They do say an an-

177

aesthetic makes one talkative, but our Eve excelled herself. She went on and on like a cracked record.'

'There appeared to be plenty to say. I would call it a verbal emetic, wouldn't you?'

They regarded one another, still feeling the ground between them.

'Did you wring Sister Trevor's neck yet, on several counts?' Laura asked, with a trembling of her lower lip.

'No.' This time he smiled. 'Some pleasures I can still anticipate.'

'She's all right, is she?'

'Eve Trevor? She will always be all right. She'll see to that.'

'I think she was trying to be nice to us.'

'I'm sorry if I can't help thinking of the Greeks, when they bring gifts.'

'And Simon. Simon's O.K., I hope?'

He looked at her as though she was slightly dimwitted, with great patience.

'I don't know whether you've noticed, Laura, but your stepson has grown used to having a mum around. He shrieked 'Mom! Mom! Mom!' at me half the night and threw his teddy at me. I wouldn't serve in the comfort stakes.'

'Jon——'

'Laura——' they spoke together, stopped and smiled wryly. 'I'll have my say out first,' Jon suggested, 'then you respond. Did I mention I have to be back in Thornsea tonight?'

'No, Jon, you didn't. All that motoring!'

'Finegan's holding the fort for me, but he goes on leave tomorrow. Now, as I see our problem, we didn't know what to expect or what was expected of us. Perhaps I was never quite fair to you. I had an advantage over you.'

'You'd been married before,' Laura said helpfully.

'I wouldn't exactly class that an advantage, any more

178

than a badly taught fiddler is congratulated by the mae-
stro he moves on to.'

'Oh,' Laura said, at a loss.

'If you'll let me continue——?' again the patience.

'Yes, of course. Sorry!'

'Where was I?'

'You had an advantage.'

'Oh, yes. Well . . .'

'Oh, no!' fretted Laura silently, for she could see
Dr Wales lumbering up to the front door. The door
pealed a merry ding dong! ding dong! 'I have to answer
the door,' she said aloud. 'I won't be a minute,' and she
closed the kitchen door after her.

'Well?' boomed the old doctor heartily, in a tone which
would notify the dead that *he* was still alive and kicking.
'And how are we today, eh?'

'Oh, much better,' Laura said quickly. 'Practically
A-1.'

'Ha, ha!' boomed her medical adviser. 'They all say
that, bless 'em, at this stage. The flat feet and varicose
veins come later. It's positive, need I add?'

'Actually,' Laura said urgently, 'my husband's here
and he doesn't know yet.'

'Oh?' the old doctor looked mischievous. 'Well, I won't
let on. Your surprise. I'd better say hello, don't you
think? May not get another chance.'

'Yes, certainly,' Laura said, in a complete flummox.
'He's in the kitchen.'

Jon rose, frowningly, at the interruption. Laura was
aware that she was twittering while the two men assessed
each other briefly.

'Well, I'll add my congratulations,' said Dr Wales,
while Laura hopped nervously from one foot to another.
'She's a good girl, is Laura. I wanted her to marry my
son, but she showed more sense.'

'I see,' said Jon, squinting down at her. 'You never told
me there was local talent, my dear.'

'Got a confinement,' Dr Wales announced lugubriously, and contrived a wink in Laura's direction. 'Must keep in practice. I'll wish you both good day.'

'Friendly call, or professional?' asked Jon, when Dr Wales had gone.

'He changed my dressings last evening. My neck felt a bit sore.'

'And today?' Jon asked in his professional voice.

'Oh, much better. No pain. It must be healing.'

'I'd like to look before I go, if you've no objection. Now we were trying to get down to bedrock on a certain subject, namely our marriage. What I wanted to say was——'

Ding dong! Ding dong!

'I give up!' said Jon in exasperation. 'Aircraft passing over, you said? This place is busier than Piccadilly Circus!'

This time Lassie came lolloping into the hall licking Laura wetly wherever she could reach.

'She seemed to know,' said one of Mrs Bradfield's friends. 'When we took our walkies she came straight here. I had to run to keep her in sight. How long are you here for?'

'Well, I don't really know——' Jon had strolled to the door to join her, and Laura made the introductions. The woman looked him over with thinly-disguised curiosity, mentally photographing him to recount his image to the rest of the village, no doubt.

'Well, I'll leave you in peace,' said Mrs Dartford. 'Bring Lassie back whenever you want to.'

'Peace!' Jon said longingly, and Lassie gave a warning growl.

'She's telling you not to be cross with me,' Laura told him. 'She senses when people are.'

'Not cross with *you*,' Jon said, 'just cross. Well, there's not much time, is there?'

'I know,' Laura said. 'You've come a long way just to be ogled by our neighbours. Don't worry. Leave it to me.' She went out to tell the young man still mowing the grass that if anybody called she would be in the bath, and then grimaced at Jon as she led the way into her father's study with Lassie wagging happily behind them. 'I've told so many white lies lately,' she shrugged. 'I'd never have believed it of myself.'

'Well, you've had a somewhat unusual pattern lately,' he excused her. 'I'm sure it's nicer for neighbours to be told you're in the bath than that you don't want to see them. Now, can I do all the talking for the next few minutes?'

'Go ahead,' she invited, wondering how she was going to feel at the end of those telling few minutes.

'When I asked you to marry me, Laura,' he began, 'I was doing something wildly impulsive for me. Of course I had a problem with Simon, but I wasn't quite honest with you. I couldn't have let him go with Bob and Kate, even if you refused me. I didn't tell you that.'

'Oh!' was torn from her.

'I suppose I would have hired a housekeeper, maybe a widow with a teenage kid who would have been glad of a home for life, because I would never otherwise have married again.'

'Then—then why did you——?' Laura piped up, but he waved her into silence and frowned.

'Your turn later,' he insisted. 'I asked you to marry me because I thought you were the most stimulating woman in the world,' he told her. 'I thought at first we were having well-matched bouts of a never-ending prize-fight, and couldn't wait to get back in the ring with you. The more this went on the better I knew I was falling in love with you, and the more I tried to resist it the harder I fell. I couldn't make enough legitimate excuses to see you. Only your natural interest in my son kept me on your dating list, I thought, and so I laid it all on a bit thick. When I asked you to marry me I really couldn't bear the thought of the lonely path you appeared to have chosen for yourself. People do dry up, you know, in time. I thought if I could share my child, with you, give you a domestic background, then I could guard you and love you, and never let anything touch you to harm you, and if nothing else happened between us that I would still be a lucky man. Of course I didn't expect you to agree, not in a thousand years, but I had to try for my own peace of mind. When you came to me, accepting my proposal, I was out of this world and yet I was telling myself, 'Watch it, Jon! Don't frighten her off. She's really taking Simon on and you just happen to be tagging along.'

'Well, it's one thing having a high-minded theory, that man and woman can live together and just be good friends. I hadn't shared a room with you long before I was a bundle of frustrations. When you came to meet me one night, in that hotel, seeking comfort and reassurance, only a ravening beast rose in me and I had to put you away from me like a naughty child. I suppose nature is always just too strong for cooler intellect, or the species would die out. Back home, when there was work, it was a bit easier, but though you graciously granted me the comfort and delight of your presence and many services, including that of coping with an uprooted child, I still had to suppress this carnal greed for you. I would eat you with my eyes when you didn't know it and I wondered if there was an anti-aphrodisiac I could take to calm myself down. Well, you, in your stately generosity, suspected my need; maybe I looked at you once too often and you read the signs; but you allowed me to love you as nature intended, and made me happier than I had any right to deserve.

'I hoped it could go on like that, but I knew I had the advantage of being in love with you, while you were still doing me a service and granting me an extra-contractual kindness. Sometimes I thought I was making you happy, and that made me feel good, but at others I fancied I was just another chore, and then I was miserable and maybe I sulked and tried to show you I could do without you. Of course I hurt myself more than anybody else. I watched you, oh, how I watched you, for signs that you were really feeling we belonged, but all I saw was the same sturdy independence not to become too involved with me. If we went out together I could circulate all evening, so could you, and did. At that wretched dance when I saw Falconer attending you, when I heard how he openly stated his feelings for you, I had to physically restrain myself from smashing his oily face in. Only you apparently responding to him stayed me. Had I any right to stop you falling in love, if you were of such a mind? You had not, after all, promised to fall in love with me when you married me. Such a thing wasn't in your province in any case. Though a third party encouraged our doubts of one another, as we now know, I must admit that I was capable of suffering agonies of jealousy with very little encouragement. I was torn between letting you have your fling and demanding your loyalty as my right.

'In all my suffering I found, to my own dismay, I was capable of small-mindedness and spite. I could only think of using Simon, of whom I know you were fond, to hurt you. What a possessive father I became when I thought you preferred someone else to me! When you decided you'd had enough I thought I understood. I had intended to keep you from becoming a dried-up old maid and I was denying you the play of these very emotions you wished to exercise, because you had discovered they could not be excercised on me. Well, I had to let you go when you reached some point of desperation. A man who hangs on to his wife when she has so obviously had enough can only become anathema to her, and I didn't want that. Of course I was shocked when you were hurt in that fire and didn't automatically turn to me. But I thought you might understand and excuse a lot if you heard the whole story from my side from the beginning. I did cheat a little and I've succeeded in making a mess for both of us.

'Now I have come to ask, humbly, what can be done? *I* can get along—somehow. I have to think of you and I want you to be happy. That's my only wish. Now I've finished having my say and it's your turn. Do you want to say anything now, or shall I leave you to think?'

Laura's colour had heightened and faded throughout this monologue. As Jon finished speaking she was very pale but composed.

'I don't think I want to say anything just yet, Jon. No!' as he stood with a kind of despairing shrug, 'no more misunderstandings, please! I want you to come for a short walk with me. After that I'll talk if you still wish me to, but there may be no need. You say you loved me,' she said as he still looked dubious and rather miserable, 'so try trusting me, will you?'

She led him out into the sunny lane, with Lassie wagging at their heels, and raised a hand in greeting to the elderly clergyman passing in an old Ford. At a crossroads stood a post box and a telephone kiosk. The signpost had four arms pointing to Banbury and Oxford, Chickory Hollow and Much Petting.

'That sounds a great place for a honeymoon,' Jon decided wryly. 'Is that where we're walking?'

'No. We're staying right here. I don't think we'll have to wait long. Ah, I thought not!'

From the village came a postman on a bicycle. He dismounted at the box, stared and then said, 'It's Laura Bradfield that was. Isn't it?'

'Yes, Mr Topping. This is my husband, Jon Warwick. That's what I wanted to see you about, actually. I just came home to get a few things, not knowing Jon was coming down, too. Well—' she looked at him—'he's always busy, like most hospital surgeons, and the fact that he could get a day off was a bit of a surprise. I wrote him a letter last evening and posted it. I know I shouldn't ask this, but could you give Jon his letter now? It contains some rather important information he should have——'

'Well, Laura,' said the postman, 'it *is* bending the rules a bit, but I know you, and I'm glad to meet your husband here. Let's see if you can recognise your letter? That it? Well, as far as I know it was never popped in the box. O.K.?'

'Thank you, Mr Topping. Now we'll go home and I'll make some lunch,' Laura told Jon.

'You'd better give me my letter,' he said, in a tight little voice. 'I take it you do mean me to read that letter?'

'Oh, yes. You can read it while I'm making some corned beef fritters. You had your say. That letter is mine.'

'Yet it was written before I arrived and you heard me?'

'Obviously. You saw me get it from Andy Topping.'

'So I presume that what you've written here stands, and you don't want to alter anything?'

'Not a word. I—I may want to add a postscript, that's all.'

He read the letter sitting on the garden seat while Laura busied herself in the kitchen. She had noticed the tin of corned beef earlier and quickly whipped up some batter and opened a tin of garden peas. There was fruit salad to follow. At least Jon wouldn't drive back to the hospital on an empty stomach.

She turned down the gas under the golden fritters as she became aware of Jon standing in the open doorway, her letter to him in his hands.

'Is—is this all really true, Laura?'

'Every word of it.'

'My God!' Suddenly they were in each other's arms, their lips met and then there was such an embracing that the breath squeezed out of her. 'Forgive me, darling!' He put at her at arm's length and surveyed her. 'You're sure there's going to be a child? *Our* child?'

'Dr Wales confirmed that this morning.'

'And you still want to put all of our futures in my hands?'

'Where better, Jan?'

He hugged her close to him again. 'How did we ever trip up, Laura? I don't get it.'

'Sit down at table and let's continue our chat. Having written so much I only have to add a few facts, but they might make you understand. We were so determined to be sensible in our marriage, Jon, that we fancied we were breaking the rules if we allowed the other to suspect we were becoming emotional. We clamped a veto on all emotional displays, and probably both went off in different directions and pounded our fists in frustration on some inanimate object. Right from the start, in that hotel room, on the occasion you mentioned, I didn't come to you for comfort and reassurance at all. I came to you as a woman to a man, and I fancied you rejected me. I didn't think you found me attractive. Later on, when we'd had a row at home, the only way I felt I could say I was sorry was to put my arms about you and not let you go until you understood I wanted to be your wife in every way. But after jumping in at the deep end, even then we didn't know enough about one another. We hadn't explored all those little by-ways of personality that lovers do, before they take the plunge. We were married and we were sleeping together, but in so many ways we were still strangers. We were in love, had we but known it, and too much strangers to be able to say it for fear of giving offence and sending the other one running. Being in love we made it into a crime. We shouldn't have done that; we were both tormenting ourselves; we hadn't allowed for anything like that. So we hurt each other, and ourselves, and other people stuck in needles and so things happened as they did.

'Yes, Jon, I did occasionally welcome Miles Falconer's company. He had known you before I did and I was greedy to hear every crumb of news about you. But as for wanting anything more of him—well! You underestimate your own attraction for a woman, Jon. I was quite prepared to believe every woman was in love with you. I didn't see how they could avoid it. I wouldn't have gone to Australia, Jon, no matter what happened. I would always have wondered about you and Simon. I might even have applied for that job as housekeeper, wearing a wig and glasses——' she dimpled and laughed for the first time in many days.

'The wig and glasses might have foxed me,' he admitted, 'but I'd know those legs anywhere. You're not exactly a stranger to these old eyes, my darling. Well!' he glanced up at the clock on the wall and looked regretful. 'I must leave in an hour,' he sighed, reaching out for her hand across the soiled platters they had used.

'*We* must leave in an hour,' she corrected.

The blue eyes brightened. 'You're coming back with me?' he asked.

'I am. I feel very happy about it, too. I don't feel I can bear you out of my sight at the moment. That may pass, with time, but I'll know, by then, that you'll always be in my life, Jon.'

'We'll have a real honeymoon in Devon, eh, darling?'

'If you sail I'll be your crew; if you fish I'll help reel 'em in. You won't be able to get rid of me. I shan't feel apologetic about wanting to be with you ever again. Oh!' she put her hand to her mouth. 'I told Cathy I had a sick relative, that I wouldn't be coming to Devon with you.'

'Well, Aunty' has a great constitution. She recovered and insisted on you keeping to your original plans. How's that?'

'Actually I have a great-aunt, and she's marvellous. Even if she was dying she'd tell me my place was with my husband.'

'Good for Great-Aunty! We must have her to stay some time, and I mean that.'

'Thank you for being so wonderful, Jon! Already we're much less strangers than we were. Now that I love you I can't wait to get to know you properly.'

'You know,' he said, speculatively glancing towards the stairs, 'we still have the best part of an hour. The honey-moon could start right here.'

'Why not?' she smiled, loving him more with every moment that passed.

Lassie cocked an ear and whined softly while her tail

thudded against the floor. She didn't understand humans and their behaviour, but she sensed her young mistress was happy and that, for any well-bred dog, was quite sufficient.

Doctor Nurse Romances

Don't miss
March's
other story of love and romance amid the pressure
and emotion of medical life.

SISTER IN CHARGE
by Judith Worthy

When Nurse Dilys Davies decides to run the nursing
home left to her in her grandmother's will she does not
expect to find the raging village feud or the unpleasant-
ness of the handsome local doctor . . .

Doctor Nurse Romances

and April's
stories of romantic relationships behind the scenes
of modern medical life are:

CHILDREN'S NURSE
by Kathryn Blair

Nurse Linda Grey travels to Portugal to look after
four-year old Jacinto but her modern ideas meet with
strong opposition from the boy's father, the handsome
Marquez de Filano.

MAJOR MIKE
by Hazel Fisher

When under Major Mike's command at the Territorial
Army camp, Nurse Lisa Hilton tries hard to ignore his
sarcastic comments, only to find she is haunted by
the Major's piercing dark eyes . . .

Order your copies today from your local paperback retailer

The Mills & Boon Rose is the Rose of Romance

Every month there are ten new titles to choose from — ten new stories about people falling in love, people you want to read about, people in exciting, far-away places. Choose Mills & Boon. It's your way of relaxing:

March's titles are:

GREGG BARRATT'S WOMAN by Lilian Peake
Why was that disagreeable Gregg Barratt so sure that what had happened to Cassandra was her sister Tanis's fault?

FLOODTIDE by Kay Thorpe
A stormy relationship rapidly grew between Dale Ryland and Jos Blakeman. What had Jos to give anyone but bitterness and distrust?

SAY HELLO TO YESTERDAY by Sally Wentworth
It had to be coincidence that Holly's husband Nick — whom she had not seen for seven years — was on this remote Greek island? Or was it?

BEYOND CONTROL by Flora Kidd
Kate was in love with her husband Sean Kierly, but what was the point of clinging to a man who so obviously didn't love her?

RETRIBUTION by Charlotte Lamb
Why had the sophisticated Simon Hilliard transferred his attentions from Laura's sister to Laura herself, who wasn't as capable as her sister of looking after herself?

A SECRET SORROW by Karen van der Zee
Could Faye Sherwood be sure that Kai Ellington's love would stand the test if and when she told him her tragic secret?

MASTER OF MAHIA by Gloria Bevan
Lee's problem was to get away from New Zealand and the dour Drew Hamilton. Or *was* that her real problem?

TUG OF WAR by Sue Peters
To Dee Lawrence's dismay and fury every time she met Nat Archer, he always got the better of her. Why didn't he just go away?

CAPTIVITY by Margaret Pargeter
Chase Marshall had offered marriage to Alex, simply because he thought she was suitable. Well, he could keep his offer!

TORMENTED LOVE by Margaret Mayo
Amie's uncle had hoped she would marry his heir Oliver Maxwell. But how could she marry a maddening man like that?

Masquerade
Historical Romances

Intrigue
excitement
romance

CHANGE OF HEART
by Margaret Eastvale

Edmund, Lord Ashorne, returned from the Peninsular Wars to find that his fiancée had married his cousin. It was her sister Anne who had remained single for his sake!

LION OF LANGUEDOC
by Margaret Pemberton

Accused of witchcraft by Louis XIV's fanatical Inquisitor, Marietta was rescued by Léon de Villeneuve – the Lion of Languedoc. How could she *not* fall in love with him, even knowing that he loved another woman?

Look out for these titles in your local paperback shop from 13th March 1981